Amy Cross is the author of more than 100 horror, paranormal, fantasy and thriller novels.

OTHER TITLES
BY AMY CROSS INCLUDE

American Coven
Annie's Room
The Ash House
Asylum
B&B
The Bride of Ashbyrn House
The Camera Man
The Curse of Wetherley House
The Devil, the Witch and the Whore
Devil's Briar
The Dog
Eli's Town
The Farm
The Ghost of Molly Holt
The Ghosts of Lakeforth Hotel
The Girl Who Never Came Back
Haunted
The Haunting of Blackwych Grange
The Night Girl
Other People's Bodies
Perfect Little Monsters & Other Stories
The Shades
The Soul Auction
Tenderling
Ward Z

CONTENTS

BROKEN WINDOW

THE HOUSE OF JACK THE RIPPER BOOK 1

PROLOGUE

Suddenly I fall, tripping on a loose floorboard and dropping to my knees. I let out a cry of pain as I tumble forward, but somehow I manage to keep my hands clamped tight against my bloodied belly.

"Matt!" I scream, trying to get to my feet but not quite summoning the strength. "Matt, run! Get out of -"

Before I can finish, I cry out in pain as more blood spills from my belly and runs between my fingers. The pain is intense, filling my mind for a few seconds as my knees buckle under my weight. I start slipping down, but somehow I manage to drag myself up.

"Matt, run!" I gasp, tasting blood in my mouth now. "Matt, you have to get out of here."

I lean against the wall for a moment and look down at my clasped hands. The cut on my belly runs all the way from one side to the other, and I can feel the weight of my intestines pushing to get out. If I move my hands away, the torn flesh will split all the way and there'll be nothing holding my guts in place. Even now, I can feel more blood seeping out between my fingers, and I think I can even see a sliver of glistening redness pushing against the cut from deep inside. And no matter how hard I try to stay up, I can't keep from sliding down once again toward the floorboards.

I adjust my hands a little, hoping to get a better grip, but the pain is intense and my fingers are covered in blood. I feel nauseous too, as if my shifting guts are trying to expel everything they contain. My underwear's soaked too. Even if I get out of here, I don't know how -

And then suddenly I hear him.

I freeze.

I don't dare look, but I know he's loose.

Letting out a groan of pain, I try again to get to my feet. This time I force myself up, but I can feel my knees trembling as if they might buckle again at any moment. I start stumbling forward, heading unsteadily toward the top of the stairs while leaning heavily against the wall. With each step, more and more blood is forced out through the cut in my belly, and when I get to the top of the stairs I let out a whimpered sob. Each step feels as if it has to be my last, yet somehow I've made it this far. I've slipped in my own blood and I've almost passed out as pain bursts through my body, but I refuse to curl up and die. I have to fight.

"Matt!" I gasp. "He's here! Run!"

I don't know where Matt is right now, but I have to find him. If he's hurt – if that monster has gotten to him – I have to make sure he's okay and get him out of here. If anything's happened to Matt, I'll never forgive myself.

I pause for a moment, leaning against the wall and letting out another groan, but then I hear a bumping sound. This time I turn instinctively, and to my horror I see the silhouette of a man standing at the far end of the landing. He's facing this way, and in his right hand he's holding a large knife with a curved blade. Even from here, I can see that blood is dribbling down onto the floorboards.

My name is Maddie Hayes, and I am not going to die like this.

"You're not going to get me," I whisper, trying to find some strength from somewhere. "I won't let you."

I lunge at the table next to the top of the stairs, desperately trying to find something I can use as a weapon. I miss the table, however, and slam against the wall, and my hands barely contain the sloughing mess that's threatening to come slopping out of my belly at any moment. I feel dizzy, and it takes a moment before I can even turn and focus on the silhouetted figure.

"Leave me alone!" I scream. "Go to hell!"

Suddenly he takes a step toward me, and he emerges from the shadows enough for me to see his dark, dead eyes.

Gripped by panic, I turn and start making my way down the stairs, but I immediately slip. I try to steady myself against the wall, but I quickly realize that I'm starting to fall. As I tumble forward, I instinctively reach out to grab the bannister, almost but not quite managing to save myself. Finally I scream as I fall. My remaining hand slips down and my intestines burst out from my belly, splattering against the bare wooden steps.

CHAPTER ONE
MADDIE

Today

“HAVE YOU SEEN ALEX? Hey, have any of you seen Alex around?”

Nobody answers.

There are two guys loading dented tin cans into an old oil drum, but other than that I don't recognize anyone down here under the bridge. It was a long shot coming here anyway, and I know Alex could be miles and miles away, but I have to at least *try* to find her.

It's been twenty-four hours now.

If I don't find her soon, maybe I never will.

This is my last shot. I spent all morning on the streets, asking anyone I could find whether they might have spotted Alex. Finally I came here, to the space under the bridge, to the place where a couple of hundred homeless people take shelter on cold and rainy nights.

The rain has passed now, leaving bright puddles in the morning light, but there are still a fair few people milling about. I know from bitter experience that people can be helpful here, but also that some can be dangerous. This is the first time I've ever been here alone, without Alex.

"Does anyone here know Alex?" I ask, stumbling slightly in the mud and then adjusting my backpack in an attempt to make it a little less top-heavy. "Does anyone here know a girl named Alex, from the house on Bowley Street?"

A woman glances at me, but she simply stares for a moment with a glassy expression before looking back down at the tattered paper coffee cup she's holding. From the look in her eyes, I half-suspect she thinks I'm a hallucination. A moment later she turns away, and I watch as she takes an unlabeled metal can and tips its contents into a bowl. Whatever's inside the can, it slops out like meat or guts, splattering the bowl.

A train rattles across the bridge above us, carrying more commuters into London. I glance up and spot silhouettes in the windows, but they're out of sight soon enough. For a moment I catch myself remembering the times when I was a little girl, when my grandparents used to bring me up on that same train for day-trips to London. I remember seeing homeless people back then, but I never thought I'd become one myself. I always thought I was safe somehow.

I can't afford to think like this right now.

I have to find Alex.

"Hi," I say as I spot another familiar face up ahead. A man, someone I think I might have seen around a couple of times before, back near the Bowley Street squat. "Sorry, but can I ask you something? Do you know a girl named Alex with a Yorkshire accent?"

The man turns to me, but there's no hint of recognition in his features.

"Do you know the Bowley Street squat?" I continue, stopping a few feet from him, careful not to get too close in case he springs a surprise. "The one that got cleared yesterday? I was supposed to meet my friend Alex there, but when I arrived there were just loads of police around. Do you know what happened to the people who were living there? Did you hear anything about where they might have gone?"

He stares at me for a moment, before turning and looking back down at the mud. It's already clear that he's not quite all there in the head, although he's still my best bet right now.

"I'm really sorry," I say, taking another step toward him, "I just really need to -"

Before I can finish, I see him slip his hand into the left-side pocket of his tattered coat. I've learned from bitter experience to be wary whenever people conceal their hands, so I immediately take a step back. The man fumbles in his pocket, and it's certainly possible that he's taking hold of a knife's handle. When I look at his face, I see that he's staring at me with wild, yellow-tinged eyes, and I quickly realize that maybe he's not going to be able to help me after all. Alex warned me about this kind of situation.

"Sorry to disturb you," I mutter, before turning and trudging away through the mud, making my way toward the spot where the riverbank starts rising up to meet the huge brick arches of the bridge.

Another train rattles past, but this time I don't allow myself to look up.

After a few more paces, I glance over my shoulder to make sure that the man isn't following me. Fortunately, he's already wandering off in the other direction. Maybe he wasn't dangerous after all, and maybe that wasn't a knife in his pocket, but I'm glad to have gotten away from him. At least for now. Alex always tells me to be careful around people I don't know, and I've learned to always listen to Alex's advice. Alex has been on the streets for a few years now. Alex knows everything.

"Maddie," a man's voice says suddenly. "Hey Maddie, what're you doing here?"

Turning, I'm surprised to see Nick sitting on his haunches just a few meters away. It must be a month since I last bumped into him, all the way over in Southfields, and I've got to admit that I'm glad to see a familiar face. As I adjust my backpack again and head over to him, I brush some strands of matted, dirty hair away from the side of my face. Tucking the strands behind my ear, I glance down at my shirt, and I immediately realize that there's no point trying to hide the fact that things haven't been going well. I'm probably still wearing the same clothes I was wearing last time I saw him, and I'm pretty sure I don't smell too good.

"It is Maddie, isn't it?" Nick asks. "From the other week?"

I nod.

Nick's okay.

Alex told me I can trust Nick, and Alex is never wrong.

"Thought so," he continues with a smile. "I never forget a face. What're you doing here? I thought you were in with those other people from Bowley Street."

"It got raided yesterday," I tell him.

"For real?"

I nod again.

"That sucks," he says with a sigh, and he seems genuinely surprised. "I was thinking of heading there myself. Do you know what happened?"

I shrug.

"More rich assholes wanting to clear people out so they can rent the place?" he adds.

I shrug again.

"It's the same story everywhere," he continues, and now there's a hint of venom in his voice. "So where were you when it happened?"

"I'd been to the station," I explain. "Liverpool Street. It was luck, really. I was supposed to meet Alex back at the house, but when I showed up..."

My voice trails off as I remember the thump of shock in my chest. I turned the corner last night, and that's when I saw all the flashing lights as police cars waited outside the house. I watched people being led out, but I didn't see Alex, which means she must have got away. Alex is smart like that. If anyone was going to slip out without getting nabbed by the police, it'd be Alex.

"I need to find Alex," I say finally. "Please, if you have any idea where she is, you have to tell me."

"Oh I do, do I?"

"Please!"

I wait for a moment, but I'm starting to realize that this conversation isn't going anywhere. Maybe Nick's just playing with me for his own amusement, so I mutter something about seeing him later as I turn to walk away.

"Okay, then," I say, feeling a little deflated, "I guess -"

"I saw her," he says suddenly.

I spin back around, and now he's pointing along the riverbank toward the park.

"About two hours ago," he continues. "I think it was her, anyway. She's got that t-shirt she always wears, right?"

"The Green Day t-shirt!" I say excitedly. "From the Revolution Radio tour!"

He nods. "Whatever. She was with some people. They looked like they were waiting for someone, and I think I heard them talking about getting some petrol from somewhere. Like, for a car or something."

"Where *exactly* was she?" I ask, and for the first time in hours I feel a flash of hope.

"I told you, she was in the park but -"

"Thank you!" I stammer, turning and hurrying away across the mud.

"Are you not gonna stay a while?" he calls after me. "Hey, I told you what you wanted to know! Don't I get anything in return?"

"I've got to find her!" I yell breathlessly, although I'm so far away now, I'm not even sure he can hear me. "Sorry, but I've got to find Alex!"

CHAPTER TWO
DOCTOR CHARLES GRAZIER

Saturday September 29th, 1888

IT'S NO USE. SHE'S DYING. As a man of science, I have to accept the truth. She's dying and it's only a matter of time before the cancer -

No.

No, she's not dying.

I shall not *let* her die.

Weakness and doubt are for other, lesser men. I must focus on the task at hand.

What I shall do, right this instant, is pull myself together. This is not the time to let doubts creep into my mind, nor is it the time to let myself be distracted. I am stronger than that. Other men might collapse into doubt at a moment such as this, but I am not like other men. I am Doctor Charles Grazier, I am the greatest surgeon in the whole of London – perhaps in the world – and I *can* do this.

The cancer's tide might be high in her body right now, but like all tides it will eventually ebb, and that is when I shall drag Catherine clear of its malign influence.

And yet...

Looking down at my hands, in which I am holding the diseased and rejected clutch of human tissue, I focus on bringing this vile weakness under control. I am an intellectual, I have an educated mind. I should not be susceptible to weaknesses of the flesh.

It takes a few minutes, but finally my hands stop shaking.

There.

I have restored order to my body. Now I must restore it to Catherine's as well. And yet, in my hands right now, I am holding the evidence of my most recent failure.

The tissue from the dead woman's uterus is now, itself, dead. There was a brief moment, up until last week, when I actually began to think that the transplant had been successful. The whore's tissue seemed to have taken to Catherine's body, in such a manner that I thought I had been proven right in all my beliefs. Perhaps it was foolish of me to allow myself to hope, but I suppose that after so many months of dread I allowed myself a moment of weakness. I began to think I had succeeded at last.

I still remember the sense of despair that I felt, last Tuesday, when I saw the first signs of necrosis. And now I have had to cut it out again, and my poor dear Catherine's agony seems set to continue. All because some dead whore could not provide healthy tissue. I went through all that trouble, catching her and killing her and harvesting what I needed, for nothing.

"Pitiless wretch," I mutter, overcome by a sense of disgust. Heading across the room, I drop the useless tissue into a metal drum. I must remember to burn the cursed thing later. "Now I shall have to -"

Suddenly I hear a bell ringing upstairs, and my heart skips a beat. I look up at the ceiling, but I already know that I have no choice. Catherine is calling me, and I must go to her.

***

"The fever will pass soon, my dear," I explain, as I slide another pillow under Catherine's head. "I'm sure you must feel dreadful, but I believe there will be no long-term harm. We must -"

Before I can finish, she clutches my wrist with a thin, bony hand. I must confess, my first reaction is to note how painfully weak she seems, and I believe I can feel the bones of her fingers pressing against me, as if her skin is now even thinner than before. Even now, after all this time, I never stop being shocked by the deterioration of Catherine's form. She grows weaker by the day.

"Are you hungry?" I ask, turning to her and seeing that her eyes are finally open.

Open and yellow, tinged with sickness. Bloodshot too.

She tries to whisper something, but her lips are

cracked and bloodied. All she manages is a faint gasp, but at the same time she grips my wrist even tighter. She is trying so desperately to say something, but the cancer will not let her.

"Do you want water?" I ask, forcing a smile as I reach over and take a cup from the bedside table. Holding the cup to her mouth, I gently tip it until some water runs onto Catherine's lips.

She keeps her mouth shut, however, and the water simply dribbles down onto the front of her nightgown.

"Perhaps later," I suggest, as I set the cup aside. "Catherine, my dear... I know you must be in a great deal of pain, and it's entirely possible that you feel as if this endeavor cannot succeed. But you must trust me, my darling, because I know that I am so very close to making a breakthrough. The tissue was wrong last time, but that does not mean the entire endeavor is in vain." I pause, before leaning forward and gently kissing her sweaty, pale forehead. "One day soon, sooner than you can imagine, you shall be well again and -"

"Kill me," she gasps.

I freeze.

"Kill me," she says again, her voice sounding a little harsher this time, yet also more urgent. "Charles, please..."

Outside, a man shouts in the street, and there's the sound of a train rumbling past in the distance. It is as if the world out there is mocking our silence here in the room.

"I know what went wrong the last time," I say

finally. "I was a fool, but as you know, I am breaking new ground with each and every procedure. I still believe the fundamental principle is -"

"Kill me..."

"I still believe the uterus to have a function in my work," I continue, "but I now also believe that tissue from the kidneys might be useful. Catherine, I have studied the necrotic tissue extensively, and I have come to the conclusion that I was simply unlucky. The donor was unsuitable, her body was filthy and diseased, but another donor would have delivered very different results."

"Charles, please..."

"The next one is going to be the charm," I add, clutching her hands tight in an effort to give her a little more hope. "I know I have said that before, and you have every reason to doubt me, but I assure you that I know what I'm doing. I spent the morning reading some of my old notes and -"

"Charles..."

"The mistake was in the initial incision," I explain, warming to my theme now as I realize that I understand where I went wrong. "Oh Catherine, once you're better and you have a little more stamina, I shall show you the whole thing. I shall talk you through it all from beginning to end. I know you'll find it fascinating once you're able to really follow the scientific process, but you mustn't worry yourself with such things right now. You need all your strength and -"

Suddenly she lets out a horrifically pained, dry gasp, and at the same time she begins to sit up in the bed. As I place my hands on her trembling shoulders, she coughs up some pale yellow slime that brings a foul, rotten stench.

"That's alright," I tell her, struggling to get her to rest. "Stay on your back, my darling. You must -"

She grabs my arm, and this time she squeezes tighter than ever.

"Charles," she gasps, with tears streaming down her face, "I'm begging you... Have mercy. It's my time. The pain is too much, I can't bear anymore. Please, just let me die."

"Your pain will end soon," I reply, and this time I manage to settle her back down against the bed. It is as if that brief burst of energy has already faded. "I promise, my darling."

"No more treatment," she whispers. "No more operations."

"The next procedure will make everything better."

"No, please..."

"My darling, you must rest."

"No more procedures, Charles..."

"You must rest and regain your strength!"

I get to my feet and take a step back. The sight of my poor, dear Catherine sobbing and trembling like this is almost too much to take. Yet deep in my heart, I know that the next operation is the one that will save her. She just needs a little faith, and soon she'll be right as rain again. She always trusted in my work before. Now she must dig deep and trust me in her darkest hour.

"Please," she gasps. "Charles, won't you show

mercy? Won't you let me go?"

She stares at me for a moment, before closing her eyes and turning her face away. I think she is still sobbing, and I cannot imagine the pain she must be going through. It is natural for her to lose hope, but I shall prove her wrong. I shall save her and make her well again. I am the great Doctor Charles Grazier, and I can do this.

"I must step out for a few hours," I tell her. "I'm sorry, but it's essential. Before I go, I shall bring up some food for you. And then, while I am out, you can rest. You understand that your suffering is going to end soon, do you not?"

I wait, but now she's simply whimpering as she continues to cry.

"Catherine?"

Again I wait, and again she does not answer.

"Everything will be alright," I continue, raising my voice to be heard over her sobs. "Wait and see, Catherine. Soon your pain will be gone, and you'll be your old self again. That, I promise."

Yet she does not answer.

She merely weeps.

Finally I turn and leave the room. Once I am out on the landing, I pull the door gently shut and then I take a moment's pause to regather my senses. It is always so awful to see Catherine like that, but I cannot hide from the truth. The last operation left her weaker than ever, and undoubtedly in more pain. I had thought that the operation was a guaranteed success, but now I see where I was wrong.

The next operation is the one that will save her. Of that, I am certain.

As I turn and head to the stairs, I can still hear Catherine's anguished, choked sobs coming from the bedroom. I do not blame her for fearing the worst, but soon she will be so much better. I just pray that she never has to know what I have done, and the lengths to which I am going, in order to save her life. I pray that she never asks where I find these fresh body parts.

CHAPTER THREE
MADDIE

Today

"ALEX!" I SHOUT, spotting her at last as I reach the top of the playground area. "Alex, wait!"

She's with some guys, heading toward a van, but she doesn't seem to have heard me. She's just walking away.

"Alex!" I shout again, waving at her before starting to run across the grass. "Alex, it's me!"

Up ahead, Alex turns and finally sees me. I race toward her, finally stopping and leaning against a tree to get my breath back. I'm exhausted after running, but at the same time I feel such an incredible rush of relief. For a moment back there, I actually began to worry that I'd never find her.

"I've been looking everywhere for you!" I gasp breathlessly, feeling a flash of pain in my chest. "Were you looking for me too? I've literally been everywhere I could think of!"

"I've been busy," she replies cautiously, and I can instantly hear a hint of detachment in her voice, as if something's wrong. "What have you been up to?"

"I've been looking for you all over the place," I explain. "I was in Mayer Street, I was all up around the back of the main park there, and down the street with all the Chinese restaurants. I looked in all the cafes, and all the places I thought you might be. I tried the park and the cafes and under the bridges and I was starting to think you'd just vanished! I couldn't decide whether it was better to stay in one place so that you'd be able to find me, or to keep racing around looking for you!"

I wait for her to reply, but she's simply staring at me.

"It's so good to see you!" I add finally, before stepping closer and giving her a big hug.

I wait for her to hug me in return, but eventually I take a step back.

"Why?" she asks finally.

"Why what?" I ask, still a little breathless.

"Why were you looking for me?"

"Alex," one of the guys says, leaning out of the van after climbing into the driver's seat, "are you coming or not?"

She turns to him.

"Give me a minute," she says, before turning back to me. "Maddie, the squat got busted."

"I know," I reply. "I got there *just* after. I saw the police going in and out, and there were already some people boarding up the doors and windows. I knew you'd made it out, though. I knew you wouldn't get dragged off."

"There's no going back there," she says with a sigh. "It was good while it lasted. It was a nice place, but these things always end. Probably some rich asshole bought it and wants to do it up so they can rent it out for loadsa money. Happens all the time, all over the city. All over the country."

"Do you know somewhere else we can go?" I ask.

I wait for a reply, but again she seems a little concerned. Skeptical, even.

"Do you?" I continue. "Alex, have you already figured out a new -"

"I'm going to Stratford," she says suddenly.

"Stratford?"

She nods.

I feel a flicker of concern in my chest.

"Why Stratford?" I ask.

She shrugs. "Dunno. 'Cause these guys are headed up there and they offered me a lift. Can't be any worse than where we've been lately. I figure I might as well give it a shot. There might be some money going."

"Sure, but..."

My voice trails off, and after a moment I see several people watching me from the back of the van. They look all ready to go, and I can't help noticing that Alex hasn't invited me yet. She will, though. She has to. Alex and I always stick together, no matter what.

"You gonna be alright, yeah?" she says after a

moment, and finally she offers a flicker of a smile. "It's been a fun couple of months. I've taught you a lot. You were such a kid when we first met, but I've really toughened you up. I know you'll be just fine on your own, Maddie."

"On my own?"

She gives me a playful punch on the shoulder.

"I believe in you," she adds. "You were a good student. And I was an excellent teacher. And these things never last forever, right?"

"Sure," I reply, and now I can feel tears welling behind my eyes. "I knew that."

"Just stick around the areas I've shown you," she continues, "and you'll be well off. There are good people here. You don't need me anymore."

"How long are you going to Stratford for?" I ask.

"Dunno. Forever, maybe. At least 'til I get some money together."

I swallow hard, still struggling to hold back the tears.

"I'd ask you to tag along," she continues, "but there's no room. There wasn't even room for me, to be honest, but they've managed to squeeze me in somehow. Sorry I was gonna split without saying goodbye, but it all came together real fast and I didn't know how to find you." She pauses, before stepping closer and placing a hand on my arm. "I'm glad you showed up, though. It's nice to say bye."

"And you're really going?" I ask.

She nods.

I swallow again. There's a lump in my throat, but I'm determined not to let Alex see that I'm scared or upset.

"Well, have fun," I say, taking a step back. "I mean, I'm sure you will. I've never been to Stratford, but I've heard it's alright. I bet you'll be fine."

"Find yourself a roof for the night, okay?"

"Don't worry about me," I reply. "I can take care of myself."

"I'd take you along," she continues, "but the guys -"

"I don't want to go to Stratford anyway," I tell her, "so I wouldn't agree. I've got things to do here."

That's sort of a half-truth. I certainly don't have any particular desire to go to Stratford, but at the same time I definitely don't want to be left here alone. I'd go if Alex offered, for sure. I'd jump into that van and I'd go with them, and I wouldn't even be scared. I'm never scared when I'm with Alex.

"Where are you gonna sleep tonight?" she asks.

"Don't worry, I'll find somewhere."

"Yeah? How?"

"I'm not an idiot," I reply, feeling a flicker of irritation. I just want to get out of here before I burst into tears. "You don't have to worry about me, Alex. I can look after myself. It's like you said, I learned a lot from you."

"Yeah, but -"

"So have fun in Stratford. Seriously. Have a nice time."

With that, I turn and start walking away, heading

across the grass. Still sniffing back tears, I at least feel relieved that I didn't break and blub in front of Alex and her new friends, although after a moment I have to wipe my nose against the sleeve of my coat. I know I shouldn't have started to depend on Alex so much, but she took me under her wing a little when I first ended up living on the streets, and I assumed we'd have a little longer together. Then again, maybe that's how things are out here. Maybe -

"Maddie."

Startled, I turn and find that Alex has followed me across the grass.

The van is still waiting, with its engine running now.

I feel a rush of hope. Maybe she's going to ask me to go with them after all.

"Where are you gonna sleep tonight?" she asks.

The hope fades. "I'll find somewhere."

"Where?"

"I don't know."

"How will you find it?"

"I'll ask around."

She stares at me, and I can see the pity in her eyes.

"I'm not a kid!" I say firmly, sniffing back tears that I know she must be able to see now. "I'm seventeen, remember? Like you said, I've gotten tougher while I've been hanging out with you."

"Yeah, but -"

"I don't need you!" I say firmly, inadvertently clenching my fists.

"Sure, I know you don't," she says with a sigh. "The problem is, you're seventeen but you look even younger, and that's not good. If you go out there, letting people know you're all alone and asking for help, sooner or later..."

She hesitates, and for a moment I actually start to wonder whether she'll promise to somehow squeeze me into that van. I swear, I'd accept.

"Remember what I taught you," she says finally, sounding a little reluctant. "Tell me the rules I told you in the beginning, Maddie. The rules about staying safe."

"I don't need your help," I lie.

"Tell me the rules."

"I remember them."

"Then tell me."

"No!" I blurt out, sounding angrier than I intended. "I don't need to!"

"You're tougher than you think you are," she replies. "I know you're probably, like, really scared right now. I'd take you with me if I could, but it's complicated. And Stratford isn't really *that* far away, so we'll probably bump into each other again. And by then, we'll both be on the up. I'm sorry we can't stick together, Maddie, but this is just how it's gotta be right now."

She puts a hand on my shoulder, but I pull away.

"I'm trying to help you," she continues.

"I think your friends are waiting," I reply, glancing past her and seeing that the others are still watching from the van. "Good luck with your new life in Stratford. I'm happy for you. Really, I am."

"Maybe I'll come back down some time," she

says. "I'll try to look you up."

"Yeah, I'll probably be back on my feet by then," I tell her, wiping away more tears. "You were right, nothing lasts forever, not on the streets. Now get going to Stratford, and don't worry about me. I'll be absolutely fine."

She sighs. "Maddie..."

I turn and walk away, although I can't help listening out for any hint that Alex is following me. When I finally get to the gate, I glance over my shoulder just in time to spot Alex climbing into the van. I loiter for a moment, with tears finally in my eyes, and I watch as the van reverses out of its spot and then drives away. I'm pleased for Alex, honestly I am, and I know I have no right to be annoyed that I wasn't invited.

She simply got a better offer, and I don't blame her for going.

And she really *is* going.

Even as the van pulls away, I can't help thinking that she might have a last-minute change of heart, that the van might suddenly pull to a halt and Alex will rush out. And then she'll either yell at me to go with her after all, or she'll let the van go and she'll tell me she's decided to stay. Alex and I have been a really good team over the past few months. I needed her, and I thought she liked hanging out with me.

Finally the van disappears from sight.

Turning, I slip out through the gate and start heading back toward the river. I'm not sure where I'll sleep tonight, but I'll find somewhere, maybe in another park. I can already see some people under the next bridge along, and they'd probably let me hang out, but right now I want to be alone. In fact, I hurry behind some bushes and drop down onto my knees, and finally all the tears come rushing out.

As I continue to sob, a train rattles across the bridge above me, taking more people into the city.

CHAPTER FOUR
DOCTOR CHARLES GRAZIER

Saturday September 29th, 1888

WHEN DID THE WORLD BECOME SO INFERNALLY LOUD?

As I step out of my front door, I stop for a moment and look down toward the street. Gas lamps have been lit and darkness is beginning to fall, but still our once-quiet part of London is filled with people. People who, it seems, feel compelled to shout and yell their every word, bringing a cacophony that I am sure must drive us all a little madder each and every day. Tradesmen are the worst, shouting at one another from opposite ends of the street, yet it seems that even respectable gentlemen are starting to make more noise. And that is before one considers the carriages that race along all day and all night, or the sounds of distant factories, or the jabber of voices that seem to reflect every language other than Her Majesty's English. London has opened its gates too wide, and now our streets are full.

It is my honest opinion that anybody who helps lower the numbers of this wretched population – howsoever they might go about this task – is doing the world a favor.

Glancing up at the house's top window, I think of my poor dear Catherine resting up there tonight, trying to get some sleep. I only hope the noise does not disturb her. In what just and fair world does such a saintly woman suffer such pain, while common idiots waste their health? Even now, Catherine tires of her struggle and slips in and out of an anguished sleep. She has so much to offer the world, yet her body keeps her trapped like an invalid. I cannot wait for the day when she finally emerges from her sickbed and resumes her role in society. Sometimes, I wonder whether her cancer is a reaction to the roughness of the modern world.

"Charles!" a voice calls out suddenly. "Good evening there! How are you doing, old man?"

Turning, I see that Doctor Thomas Culpepper has stopped at the garden gate with his wife just a few paces behind. He is grinning at me in that rather inane manner that I remember so vividly from our years together at the hospital on Slocombe Street. Truth be told, I had hoped that I would not see the man again after I retired, yet it seems I bump into him more and more. I do not wish the man ill, but I long for the day when he finally leaves me alone.

Still, one must be polite to one's peers.

"I haven't seen you in a while," he continues as I make my way toward the gate. "It must be, what, three or four weeks?"

"Indeed."

"We have been busy dealing with the aftermath of a break-in," he explains. "We were the latest victims of this child thieves who are sent out from the slums to steal from the houses of good people."

"I have heard of such things," I reply. "There have been no cases in this area yet, but I am sure they are coming."

"Disgusting little wretches," Culpepper mutters. "If it were up to me, I would burn the slums down."

"And what of the poor children?" his wife asks.

"Let them burn too," he says proudly. "They have nothing to offer the world. They're just homeless, pointless little thugs who enjoy being part of these criminal gangs. Burn the slums, I say, and burn those who made them too."

"Harsh words," I point out, "for a man who has worked with sick children."

"The children of my esteemed clients," he replies, "are hardly to be compared to the wretched orphans that infest the slums."

I glance at Culpepper's wife Delilah, and I fancy I see a little discomfort in her features, as if she does not agree with her husband. Still, as a good wife, she knows better than to contradict him.

"I always forget, Charles," Culpepper continues, "that you live on Cromwell Road. Still, these little meetings are a pleasant surprise for both us, aren't they?

It's always nice to see a friendly face. I was just telling Delilah that I hadn't seen you in a while, and she reminded me that just because you're retired now, that doesn't mean you have nothing with which to fill your days."

"Indeed," I say again, as I nod at Culpepper's wife.

She smiles demurely. It is good to see a woman who knows her place.

Stepping out to join the pair of them on the pavement, I take a moment to slip my hands into my gloves.

"And how are things going?" Culpepper asks, with a sudden note of caution in his voice. "How's Catherine?"

"Catherine is very well," I reply carefully, hoping that this simple answer might be the end of the discussion. Then again, Culpepper has never recognized subtleties.

"But has her -"

"She is recuperating as we speak," I add, keen to avoid a lengthy discussion on the matter. Evidently news of my wife's illness has reached the smoking clubs, at least. "Soon she will be up and about, and as healthy as ever."

"Really?" He furrows his brow. "I was under the impression she was rather more gravely ill than that."

"You can tell her that yourself," I reply, "when next you see her out and about. Mark my words, she *shall* be fit and healthy in time for this year's ball at the Ambassador."

"Is that so?" he replies, and I can hear the skepticism in his voice. Or is it pity? Does he believe me to be misguided and delusional? "Well, one must hope so, mustn't one? One must remain hopeful."

"It is more than hope," I say sternly. "It is knowledge, based on science. I did not think you to be a man who relies on such things as hope, Doctor Culpepper. Hope is for those who have no evidence. I have evidence, and that evidence shows that Catherine is recovering."

"That's remarkable," he replies, "quite remarkable. I should like to know more about her treatment some time. Perhaps, Charles, you have stumbled upon something that could be of benefit to the rest of us."

"You'll have to excuse me," I tell him. "I have somewhere to be, and I cannot stay out for too long. I'm sure you and your wife have somewhere to be."

"Of course, old man." He pats me on the shoulder. "Be careful where you walk at night, though. Perhaps this Jack the Ripper fellow has a thing for gentlemen as well as ladies. I was just telling Delilah that we must all be on our guard."

Having already turned to walk away, I hesitate for a moment before turning back to him.

"What are you talking about?" I ask.

"Jack the Ripper," he continues. "You heard about the letter, did you not?"

"I have no idea what you mean."

"Have you not been paying attention to the newspapers?"

"I have had a lot on my mind," I reply, feeling a flash of concern in my chest. "I can't be expected to keep up with the trivial concerns of the masses. They're always getting hot and bothered about one thing or another." I hesitate, knowing full well that I should simply walk away, yet something about Culpepper's countenance makes me feel I should ask a little more. "But tell me," I continue, "what exactly is this Jack the Ripper business?"

"It's the man who killed those women," he explains. "You know the ladies of the night who were found butchered and mutilated? You won't believe this, but apparently the killer sent a letter to one of the news services and, well, he seems to have gained this rather ghastly nickname. Now, people *are* saying it might be a hoax, but you never know, do you? I mean, what kind of person would lie about such things?"

He steps closer, and it's clear from his expression that he finds this business rather exciting. He is precisely the type of gullible, sensation-loving cretin who would sit slathering and dribbling over the pages of the gutter press.

"The madman signed the letter himself with the name Jack the Ripper," he continues, lowering his voice to a conspiratorial hush. "Can you believe such a thing? I suppose he took the name because of the way he ripped those poor women apart, but it's still rather macabre. Of course, I wouldn't put it past the news agencies to make the whole thing up, just to sell some more papers. Then again, there are some nasty people in London of late, are there not? One doesn't really know what to think!"

"The city is certainly crowded," I reply, although in truth my head is rushing. Why would anyone have written to the newspapers and attempted to take credit for the murders of those two whores? Is this some form of sick joke?

"There have been scores of letters," Delilah adds, as if she believes it is somehow appropriate for a lady to speak of such things. "As many as three a day, is what I heard."

"Most of those are written by lunatics," Culpepper points out.

"But what if some of them aren't?" she asks. "What if even one of them is genuine?"

"Everyone's talking about what's going on," Culpepper continues. "I was at the club earlier, and the place was abuzz. Everyone seems to have their own theory about who this madman might be. In fact, there are so many different ideas going around, one can hardly keep track. The one I've heard the most is that the killer might be Jewish."

"Some of the ladies think he might be Polish!" Delilah interjects. "Apparently they can be quite forceful!"

"Whoever he is," Culpepper continues, "he's running rings around the police, and now perhaps he's even taken to taunting them. I mean, honestly, what sort of person adopts a moniker like Jack the Ripper? It's so obscene and disgusting, one can hardly even comprehend that it's true. I've barely stopped reading about it all day!"

"Nor have I!" Delilah adds, her eyes wide with

wonder. "It's all I can think about!"

"Then perhaps you would do well to ponder other matters," I reply. "It cannot do the mind of a gentleman any good, it might even cause harm, if he thinks too much of these awful crimes. And as for a lady, well, I cannot imagine how you are affected by such awful stories, Mrs. Culpepper!"

"I read Thomas's newspapers as soon as he sets them down!" she replies.

"It's true," Culpepper says earnestly. "She damn near snatches them from my hands!"

"I try to be patien," she continues, "but it's so difficult!"

"Of course," he adds, "I tell her to protect herself from the nastier aspects of the story, but she doesn't listen."

"No," she says, "I don't. The last victim had her uterus removed. They say her throat was cut wide open, with two large slashes that ran from ear to ear and -"

"I must go!" I announce firmly. "I do not wish to discuss such terrible things, and I would advise you to put them from your mind. We are gentlemen, Culpepper, and we do not indulge ourselves in the petty squabbles and miseries of this sordid world. We have a duty to remain above such madness. We also, I would remind you, have a duty to keep such tales from reaching the ears of ladies. And now, if you do not mind, I really must get to my club."

"Of course ," he replies, and now he sounds suitably chastened. "I don't know what I was thinking of, really. You're right, Charles. One mustn't allow oneself to become too engrossed in the details of these awful murders. Let us simply hope that the killer is caught soon and hung."

"In public, I hope," Delilah adds.

"I must go," I say again, turning and walking away.

As I make my way to the street corner, I have a terrible fear that the Culpeppers will come running after me and attempt to continue the conversation. If they were to follow me all the way to Channing Street, I would have to actually go to the club, but fortunately I glance over my shoulder and see that they are walking in the other direction, and that they are already deep in conversation. Finally, the imbeciles have understood that I have no interest in their prattling nonsense, and I can only hope that I shall not bump into them again any time soon.

Stopping at the corner, I am about to cross when I spot a maid carrying a basket of sheets into an alley at the side of a house.

For a moment, as she slips into the darkness, it occurs to me that she must be all alone in that alley, and that I could go after her easily enough and perhaps get tonight's business out of the way.

Then again, I know I should not be too brazen, and that it would be madness to commit such an act within striking distance of my own home. When I began this nasty business, one of the first rules I set for myself was that I shall always journey a little way from the house.

It is further into Whitechapel that I must go, to

Hell itself, and there I shall find another whose death will allow my dear Catherine to live.

CHAPTER FIVE
MADDIE

Today

"DO YOU WANT SOME?" a guy asks, turning to me and holding something out in his hand. "It's not a trick. It's food."

I watch him for a moment, as he sits silhouetted against the fire that's burning in the old oil drum, but then I shake my head. Ever since I came under the bridge a little while ago, I've been aware that people have noticed me, although I've kept myself to myself. The last thing I want is to talk to anyone, and I'm pretty sure I still have teary eyes. I want to be near people, but I want to be left alone.

"Too good for it, are you?" he continues.

"I'm not hungry."

He laughs, before turning and dropping the scrap of food into his mouth. Whatever it was, I wish I'd been able to accept, but I don't quite trust these people. Down here, when someone gives you something, they always want something in return. I don't have much to give, but I'm sure they'd come up with a few ideas. Alex once told me that there are certain ways for girls to gain favor, and she made me promise I wouldn't ever go down that route. I might be hungry, but I'm not *that* hungry.

Not yet.

Anyway, I'm too busy coming up with a plan. Tomorrow I'm going to keep walking east, and I think I should eventually get to Charlton. I remember hearing about a few other people heading that way in the past, and there's supposed to be a decent number of squats in the area. If I can find somewhere a little more permanent to sleep, maybe I can start figuring out what to do next. There has to be some kind of shelter I can eventually get into, one where they'll guarantee to never, ever contact my parents. Unfortunately, Alex says there's no way I can be sure of that, not until I turn eighteen. I just have to wait until my next birthday before I try to get proper help.

As I pull my backpack a little closer, I hear footsteps coming this way, and I turn just in time to see that the guy from earlier is now coming this way. I instantly flinch and start trying to work out which way I can run.

"I've got some good food here for you," he says, stopping a few feet away and towering above me. "Why don't you want it?"

"I'm okay, thanks."

"You're not hungry?"

I shake my head.

"That's a lie," he continues. "Do you know how rude it is to turn down food?"

"I'm not being rude," I tell him, "I just -"

"Are you worried I'll want something in return?"

I open my mouth to reply, before realizing that maybe this conversation would be best left abandoned. Clutching my backpack, I stumble to my feet. Alex always told me to leave any situation in which I feel uncomfortable.

"Sorry," I mutter as I turn and start walking away.

"Stuck-up bitch!" the guy yells after me. "Get out of here! Who said you could sit near us, anyway? Go find some other people to bother! I wouldn't give you a scrap of anything, not even if you got down on your knees and begged!"

I don't look back. Instead, I keep walking until I reach the gate that leads into the park, and then I start making my way across the grass. I don't like this park, and Alex always warned me to avoid places where there's no lighting. She even warned me about this specific park, 'cause apparently some bad things have happened here in the past, but she also told me that sometimes you have to take a risk or two. Right now this is my best route, and I'm sure I'll be fine.

I set off around the park's perimeter, keeping close to the railings. After a moment, however, I spot something moving in the distance, over in the darkness near the farthest gate. I pause for a few seconds, worried that somebody might be watching me, and then I take a few steps over to the treeline. At least here I have some extra shadows for cover, and I wait for a few minutes, just in case there's any hint that I might not be alone.

Even though I'm making quite a bit of noise as I traipse between the trees, I'm pretty sure it'll only take me a few minutes to reach the other gate. Glancing around as I walk, I keep listening out for any sign that somebody might be coming closer, but with each step I start to relax a little more. This isn't the first time I've spooked myself and it won't be the last, and I'm just going to have to keep repeating the same two words that have become my mantra lately:

Toughen up.

Reaching a path that runs through the forest, I slow and look both ways before crossing. There's no sign of anyone, although the darkness is impenetrable. The only light is a faint orange glow behind some of the trees, caused by the city, and I can't even see any stars in the night sky.

Adjusting my backpack, I slip between the trees on the path's other side, determined to -

Suddenly something slams into me from behind, shoving me into a tree and then hauling me down by my shoulders. I land hard on my chest and cry out, but an arm quickly wraps around my throat and pulls tight, almost cutting off my airway.

"Where've you been, huh?" a familiar voice hisses into my ear, as I feel a hand starting to pull my trousers down from behind. "Did you find your buddy?"

I try to cry out, but he quickly moves his right hand to cover my mouth, while his left hand forces my underwear down. As I struggle, I can hear the jangling of his belt as he gets himself into position, but he seems to be having trouble and after a fraction of a second I feel his grip loosening just slightly. He's muttering to himself and he sounds annoyed about something.

This might be my only chance.

Somehow managing to twist around, I swing my right fist toward his face. He cries out and falls back, and I try to pull away. He's already coming back at me, however, so I roll onto my back and pull my knees up to my chest before kicking as hard as I can. Even with my pants around my ankles, I manage to hit him square in the face, and he once again slumps down onto the dark grass.

I remember Alex telling me to run if I ever get attacked. Never try to fight back, always run, so I pull my trousers up and scramble to my feet, but the guy is already getting up too.

I turn away, but suddenly I feel a hand on my shoulder and then I'm pulled back.

Just as I'm about to cry out for help, I feel the cold metal of a knife's blade slicing into my waist from behind. I fall against the tree, wincing with pain, and a moment later the blade slides out again. Already, warm blood is dribbling down to the top of my pants, and I'm starting to tremble with shock. I don't know how deep the knife went, but the pain is incredible and I instinctively grip the tree's damp bark, digging my fingernails deep in an attempt to keep from collapsing.

"Now why'd you make me go and do that?" the voice asks. "I wasn't gonna hurt you! I just wanted something!"

I try to turn to him, but my backpack slips partway off my shoulders and I'm already starting to feel weak. I open my mouth to cry out, but somehow no words come from my throat. It's almost as if the sheer shock of the knife wound has made me lose my mind. Even though I'm still digging my fingers into the tree, I can feel my knees weakening and I'm terrified I might be about to fall.

I think maybe the knife went deeper than I realized.

"This could have been nicer," the voice says, as the guy steps closer. "It could've been a nice moment between two lonely people. Now you're making it all unpleasant. Why've you gotta do that, eh? What's the point of being a little -"

Crying out, I swing my backpack at him, somehow summoning the strength from somewhere and hitting him on the side of the head, sending him sprawling away into the darkness. Without waiting to see whether he's hurt, I turn and run, somehow managing to keep hold of my backpack as I race between the trees. I don't dare look back, I don't dare slow; I just run as fast as I can manage, pushing through the pain as I race through the darkness. Holding my hands out to make sure that I don't slam face-first into a tree, I let out a series of pained gasps as I almost trip and almost stumble several times.

Any second now, he could grab me from behind again and pull me back, and I think this time I'll be powerless to stop him. I just have to keep running and pray that I get away, even as I feel more warm blood soaking into my trousers.

CHAPTER SIX
DOCTOR CHARLES GRAZIER

Saturday September 29th, 1888

A SCREAM RINGS OUT AND I TURN, just in time to see a woman run from a nearby house. As she scurries past me, I realize she's laughing, and a moment later a man rushes from the house with his trousers around his ankles. He mutters something crude to me and sets off after the woman, and they quickly disappear into the darkness of the night.

The people in this part of London are rotten to their core, and beyond salvation.

Setting off again along the street, I cannot help but think back to the Whitechapel of my youth. There was a time when this area was pleasant and well-ordered, when a gentleman would think nothing of coming to spend a few hours in its clean streets. Now, however, the place is infested with people who have flocked to London, and one can barely leave Whitechapel Road for a few meters in any direction without coming across some sign of squalor. It is popular to blame the Irish, but in truth it seems to me that the problem is not any one group; rather, it is the fact that so many people, from so many different walks of life, have been crammed together in such a small space. Whitechapel has become, over the past decade or so, an intolerable blight. Even Dorset Street was once tolerable.

And yet this squalor has its uses, for Whitechapel is now the kind of place where one can find people whose lives do not matter. Whores and opium addicts, liars and murderers and gamblers. Whitechapel is where the godless congregate, and nobody – not even the esteemed Doctor Barnardo or the guileless Mr. Booth – could ever hope to help these wretches. The people here are human flotsam, with no redeemable qualities whatsoever. In this sense, then, they serve some kind of useful purpose.

Stopping in a doorway for a moment, I listen to the sound of some nearby drunks. These people consume alcohol by the gallon, with no aim other than to numb their senses and obliterate their minds, and one would have to be a very charitable man to consider their lives to have any value at all.

I am not a charitable man tonight.

Suddenly a pony comes past, pulling a man on a two-wheeled cart. I pull back into the shadows of the doorway a little more and wait for the cart to leave, and then after a moment I realize that the carousing drunks seem to have moved on as well. My heart is pounding now, as is always the case when I come out in search of human organs, but I know I must act quickly and decisively. I have come out for organs on five previous occasions, and only twice did I actually succeed. Tonight, however, I have absolutely no choice.

I need a uterus, and two kidneys, and perhaps part of a liver as well. If I fail, Catherine might not last another day.

Once I am sure that the street is clear, I hurry out and make my way to the far corner. Already, I can hear the sound of men singing in one of the nearby buildings, and I soon see that some kind of event seems to be taking place in the club for working men. Socialists and Jews, I shouldn't wonder. I had hoped to find the streets empty this late at night, but I suppose in Whitechapel one can never be too far from large groups of people. Stopping near the club, I look around and see that nobody seems to be in the immediate area, but one never knows whether one is being watched.

Suddenly hearing footsteps, I glance over my shoulder and spot the silhouette of a policeman at the far end of the street. My heart skips a beat as I watch the silhouette stop for a moment, and his head turns as if he is looking this way. And then, just as I worry that I must beat a hasty retreat, the officer turns and walks away, ambling out of sight as he continues his pointless patrol.

It is good that I saw him, for now I can be sure he will not be back in this street for at least fifteen minutes. Perhaps longer.

A moment later, hearing somebody cough, I turn

and see that a whore is standing near the door to the club. She's shuffling on her feet, although after a few seconds she glances at me and I can immediately tell that she thinks I might be her next customer. She looks to be in her forties, and reasonably fit, and she is trying to make herself seem more attractive by standing straight and arching her back. Already, I can tell that she will be fine for my purposes, and I glance around to check that nobody is watching.

My heart is beating so fast and so hard, I can feel it pounding in my chest.

Once I am sure that I am not under observation, I make my way over to the woman, who in turn has begun to smile at me. There are voices shouting in the distance, and I still hear songs being sung in the nearby club, but nobody seems to be watching as I stop next to the woman.

"How much?" I ask, although the words catch a little in my throat. Reaching into my pocket, I take out some coins and show them to her. "Is this enough?"

"Depends what you want," she replies with a grin and a broad, perhaps Scandinavian accent, before taking the coins and examining them. "These'll definitely get you something."

She slips the coins into her pocket and reaches out, taking my hand in hers. Her fingers are rough and covered in callouses, and my first instinct is to pull away. Instead, however, I let her lead me along the street and then through the open gate of an unlit yard. Now I can barely see at all, although the light of the moon at least allows me to make out the whore's shape as she walks. She is well-built and stocky, which I suppose to be a sign of reasonable health.

"Got anything in mind?" she asks, stuttering slightly. "Anything particular?"

"What do you mean?" I reply, playing for time.

"You're a gentleman, aren't you? What's a gentleman doing out here at such a late hour? Feeling lonely, are you?"

"I do not know," I stammer, as I reach into my pocket and take out a knife. In this bad light, the whore will not see what I am holding, although I am starting to worry that I shan't be able to see what I'm doing when I remove her organs. I would prefer to have good light for what I am about to do, but at the same time I know that darkness is my greatest ally. "I would rather go elsewhere," I add. "Somewhere with a little illumination."

"You want to see what you're doing, do you?"

"It would be helpful."

She stops and turns to me, and she's already giggling as she starts to lift her skirt.

"Here'll have to do," she continues. "Don't worry, you'll have a fine time. I've not been encumbered with children, you see. Makes a difference, that. To a lady's parts, I mean. You'll find me tight, and who knows? You might even become one of my regulars. Often they do."

"Turn around," I reply, keen to get this over with. Her stuttering is beginning to annoy me.

She grins, before turning away and starting to lift her skit higher, exposing her bare posterior.

"Now," she continues, parting her buttocks as I step up behind her, "don't -"

Suddenly I grab her and pull her back. She lets out a gasp, and then she starts to laugh, but I know I have to strike fast so I slash the knife across her neck. To my shock, however, the blade merely catches in the fabric of a handkerchief.

I quickly clamp my hand over her mouth, to keep her from crying out, and then I pull on the handkerchief and force the struggling woman to the ground. Her laughter has stopped and now she is panicking, clearly having realized that I mean her harm. Although she has a firm and strong build, I am able to contain her attempts to break free, and her muffled cries are certainly not loud enough to draw attention. I can still hear men singing in the club nearby as I pull the handkerchief aside and re-position the knife.

Let the fools sing.

"This is for the benefit of a good woman," I whisper, slicing the blade deep into the whore's throat and cutting from left to right. I immediately feel blood erupting from the wound and running over my fingers. "Better than you. Your death will save her."

Again, she tries to cry out.

"There there," I continue, "you do not need to understand. Just trust me. This is how it has to be. Quiet now, and let me focus on my work."

She struggles desperately, but in the darkness I can already feel that she has lost a great deal of blood. She tries to bite my hand, but to no avail. I twist the knife a little, making sure to cut deep enough that the matter will be over quickly, and then I pull the blade away and simply hold the woman tight as her death throes continue. To her credit, she manages to kick my ankle and cause me a little pain, but finally she starts to weaken and I feel the sudden shift in her weight as she loses consciousness.

I wait a moment longer, just to be sure, and then I carefully move my hand away from her mouth.

She is dead.

I start rolling her over, but in truth this yard is far too dark. I did not think the matter through properly, and it is evident now that I shall have to remove her to some other place before I cut her abdomen open and begin to harvest her organs. My mind is racing as I try to work out where I can take her, but I do not know this particular area well enough. I have killed the whore, but now there is a danger she will be wasted if I do not find some light. I have to think fast, since it is imperative that I remove the organs as quickly as possible.

Suddenly hearing the sound of a pony and cart, I glance over my shoulder, and to my horror I see that some fool is driving straight into this very yard. Filled with panic, I hesitate for a moment before letting go of the dead whore's body and stepping back. With any luck, this idiot will simply leave again, although a few seconds later I hear him talking to the pony, asking the cursed animal why it is acting so strangely as it comes to a halt.

"Go away," I whisper under my breath. "Leave us alone."

I hear the sound of the man stepping down from

his cart, followed by the sound of footsteps.

"Go away!" I hiss. "Just let me get on with my work!"

"What's up with you, old thing?" he mutters, speaking with a strong foreign accent. "What's got your knickers all in a twist?"

I hear him slapping the pony's side, followed by the sound of him taking a few steps closer across the dark yard. Evidently he is in no mind to leave. Indeed, if anything, he seems to be set upon the idea of checking the yard.

Why must people be such busybodies? This man is clearly a common working idiot, and he has no place interrupting the work of his betters.

Stepping back, I wait for this idiot to leave. Every second that he's here is another second that I am denied the chance to perform my work. The dead whore's organs will have already begun to deteriorate, and I'm starting to think that perhaps I shall have to kill this man. In fact, as I tighten my grip on the knife's handle, I realize that there is no point in being weak here. I have not killed a man before, but it is clear that he must die.

Suddenly he lights a match, bringing a flickering light to the yard, and I see the horrified look on his face as he spots the dead woman on the ground. He stares for a moment, as if he cannot comprehend what he is seeing, and then he turns and runs.

"Murder!" he calls out. "There's been a murder! Police! There's been another murder!"

And in the distance, sure enough, other voice

start shouting too.

CHAPTER SEVEN
MADDIE

Today

BREATHLESS AND BLEEDING, finally unable to force my body to keep going, I slam against a low wall and almost tip all the way over. Steadying myself for a moment, I wince as the pain tears up from my waist, and then I turn to look back along the street.

I wait.

There's no sign of him.

I watch the parked cars, just in case I spot a figure coming this way. It's hard to believe that I could outrun the bastard, especially while I'm bleeding so heavily, but after a few seconds I realize that there's no reason why he'd be hiding. If he was still coming, he'd have grabbed me by now and he'd be doing whatever he wanted to do to me.

Still struggling to get my breath back, I lean

against the wall, steadying myself against the backpack. My lungs are screaming with pain and my heart is pounding, but after a moment I reach down and touch the area where the knife sliced into my waist. Immediately, I feel blood all over my skin, running from the wound to the top of my trousers. I don't dare touch the cut itself, since the pain will be too strong, but I can already tell that the wound isn't quite as deep as I first feared. Still, I've lost a fair amount of blood.

If I go to a hospital, they'll find out my name and home address.

And then, since I'm still technically a kid, they'll call my parents.

Wincing, I start stumbling along the street. I have to keep hold of the low wall, supporting myself carefully, and my knees are starting to feel weak. I'm terrified that I might collapse at any moment, and that's something I can't afford. If I collapse I'll eventually be found by someone, and then I'll get taken to a hospital. And if *that* happens, the same problem rears its head.

They'll find out my name somehow, and my address.

Then they'll realize I'm a kid.

And then they'll call my parents.

Biting my bottom lip as I feel the pain burning through my waist, I reach the street corner and stop again. Looking around, I realize that I'm somewhere near Aldgate, which means I must have run further than I realized. I know this area pretty well, but I don't know anyone who might be able to help me. Alex would know what to do, but I guess I have to get used to the fact that

Alex isn't around anymore. After struggling on for a few more steps, I stop and lean against the wall, but this only makes the pain feel ten times worse. Still, I need to rest for a moment, so I lean forward and try to gather my thoughts.

My heart is pounding, and for a moment I feel as if I'm about to collapse.

And then I see the street sign on the other side of the road, and I feel my blood run cold.

Cromwell Road, E1.

I'm in Whitechapel.

I've been on this very street before, long ago with Alex.

I look along the dark street, and I immediately see that only two or three of the streetlights are actually working. There are cars parked all the way along, but I don't see any sign of movement. I guess it must be well past midnight now, so most people are asleep. There are lights in the windows of a few nearby houses, but they look mostly like the kind of lights people leave on when they go to bed.

Forcing myself to get going again, I start limping along the pavement. My backpack feels so much heavier than before, and I don't even know how I manage to keep going. I have to steady myself for a moment against a bus stop, but finally I stumble and hobble a few more meters before stopping and seeing that one particular house on this street has been left in absolute darkness, with boarded-up windows and an overgrown front garden. If I didn't know better, I'd swear that the trees and bushes are trying to cover the house completely and keep it from being seen.

Number nine, Cromwell Road.

How's that for a coincidence? I ran desperately from the park, and of all the places in London, I've ended up right outside the one house that Alex warned me about when we walked past a few months ago. Even now, I can hear her warning ringing in my memory.

"See that place?" she told me. "Never go in there. Even if it's the last house in the whole goddamn city, do *not* go inside."

I remember being curious. "Why not?"

"Everyone knows not to go in there, Maddie. Even the most desperate assholes on the street. There's just something evil about the place."

"Evil?"

I remember being surprised. Alex was always very calm and rational, but that day she talked about the house as if she genuinely believed it possessed some other kind of quality. She was being pretty mysterious, too, which wasn't like her at all.

"Can't you feel it?" she asked, as we stopped right out here on the street in broad daylight. "Can't you feel the evil emanating from the house itself?"

I couldn't. "Not really."

We stood in silence for a moment.

"Can you?" I asked.

"Hell, yeah," she replied, surprising me. "There are stories about this house. Too many to keep track of. But all you have to remember, Maddie, is that you must never, *ever* go inside. No matter how desperate you might get."

It's a pretty crazy coincidence that after all these months, I happen to be right outside that house again. And whereas last time I was here in the middle of the day, now it's a little after midnight and all I see before me is a vast black shape silhouetted against a starless sky.

Limping to the gate, I look up at the windows. As my eyes adjust a little more to the darkness, I see that the house has three storeys, each with bay windows, but I also see that there are wooden panels covering the glass panels. Even from here, I can see that there's some kind of security device fitted over the front door, most likely to deter looters and squatters. The house itself looks pretty decent, and there's no obvious sign of vandalism. There isn't even any graffiti on the wooden panels, which is something of a miracle. In fact, the whole house looks to have been left completely alone, ignored by the rest of the world. The houses on either side have long, tall fences, as if their occupants want to keep themselves to themselves, but the detached number nine looks completely untouched.

I reach out to open the front gate.

"Never go near that place, Maddie," I hear Alex's voice saying in the back of my mind. "I'm warning you now. One of the most important lessons you can learn on the streets of London is that you never, ever go inside number nine, Cromwell Road. Not even if your life depends on it."

I let my hand rest on the gate for a few seconds, as I feel a few spots of rain on the back of my neck.

"Come on, let's get going," I remember Alex

saying, tugging on my arm and leading me along the street. "I don't even like being *this* close. That house has a weird vibe."

I've never, ever gone against Alex's advice before.

I turn to walk away, but at that moment a shooting pain ripples up my right leg and I flinch. Stopping to lean against the wall for a moment, I stay completely still, terrified that the pain might return at any moment. I don't know how many cuts and bruises I sustained earlier, other than the knife wound to my waist, but I really need a place to curl up for a few hours. I'm sure I'll be fine, but I can't be out on the street like this for too long. Eventually somebody's going to notice me, and they'll see that I'm hurt, and...

I've got to face facts. The longer I'm out here, the bigger the risk that somebody'll try to help. And help means contacting my parents.

Suddenly I hear a brief set of footsteps somewhere nearby.

I turn and look back the way I came. The footsteps have already stopped and I don't see anyone, but I swear I heard five or six clear, distinct steps coming this way.

My heart is pounding again, and I'm terrified that the guy from the park might finally have caught up.

Turning again, I see that a dark, narrow alley runs between numbers nine and seven. The scene doesn't look particularly appealing, but then neither does the street. I hesitate for a moment, weighing up my options, before finally realizing that the least worst choice is probably all I have left. Slowly, and with pain in my arms and waist and legs, I turn and start limping along the alley.

CHAPTER EIGHT
DOCTOR CHARLES GRAZIER

Saturday September 29th, 1888

MY HANDS ARE SHAKING AS I HURRY ALONG THE STREET. I can hear the shouts and cries of an excited crowd in the distance, as more and more foolish locals flock to the yard. Evidently the people of Whitechapel wish to see what has happened, and the discovery of the whore's corpse has caused quite a commotion.

"There's been another murder!" a woman's voice shrieks nearby.

"Hurry!" a man adds. "They've found someone in Dutfield's Yard!"

"It's horrible!" another woman squawks.

I hurry onward, listening to the voices that echo all around.

Finally, once I am sure that I have put enough

space between myself and the yard, I stop in another doorway and look at my gloved hands. I am shaking terribly, as if some inner fear has taken possession of my body. No matter how hard I try to calm myself, I find that my hands are jerking violently of their own accord. Never before did I think that I could be so startled, and that my body could refuse to obey the orders of my mind. Yet that moment of discovery in the yard earlier – when I was so nearly caught in the act – has shaken me to my core.

I could have been arrested.

The idiot cart-driver turned and ran before spotting me, but that in itself was a miracle. *Another* miracle was the fact that I managed to slip away before anybody else came to see what was happening. I am not an athletic man, nor am I as quick on my feet as I might have been when I was younger. I quite feel that I was blessed tonight, that some divine force was guiding me and ensuring that I did not end up in a jail cell. I have always known that there are risks involved in what I'm doing, but this is the first time that I have actually come so very close to being apprehended. It takes a few more seconds before I am able to put all thought of divine intervention safely out of my mind.

"Calm down," I whisper, still trying desperately to control my trembling hands. "You are an intellectual. You have self-control."

And yet nothing works. My hands are shaking, perhaps worse than ever, and I cannot help imagining what would have happened if I had been caught tonight. I'm quite certain that even the miserable cretins at

Scotland Yard would have eventually connected me to the two previous killings, and my noble intent might well have failed to convince the police to let me go. They would not understand that the life of my dear Catherine is worth more than the lives of one hundred – no, one thousand – Whitechapel whores, and the pathetic social reformers would undoubtedly have piled in to demand so-called justice. If the police had caught me, I would surely have ended up at the gallows.

Closing my eyes, I try to find some source of calm in my soul.

Finally, after several minutes, my hands stop shaking. Whether this is due to my brief meditation, or whether the infernal engine in my body has merely slowed, I cannot tell. All that matters, I suppose, is that I once more have myself under control.

It is late now, well past 1am, and I should be home by now. Catherine – if she is awake – will be starting to wonder where I am. I can hear shrieks and cries in the distance, and the police are no doubt all over the yard by now. I step out of the shadows and hurry along the street, heading away from the noise. I want nothing more than to go home and recover, yet at the same time I know that I must acquire certain organs tonight. As I pass a local synagogue, however, I feel that my thoughts are too disordered for me to be able to get anything done. Perhaps I shall have to wait until tomorrow, even if this means another night of agony for my dear Catherine.

And then, stopping at the end of the street, I see the most perfect and unimaginable gift.

A woman is making her way into a small square. She appears unsteady on her feet, as if she has been drinking. I watch as she walks, and I listen to the sound of her footsteps echoing in the night air, and already I am starting to feel as if fate has guided this wretch into my path.

No, not fate.

I do not believe in fate.

This is merely good fortune, balancing out the ill fortune I experienced a few minutes ago.

I watch as the woman disappears from view, and then I quickly hurry across the street, stopping again when I see her crossing the square. The scene is almost perfect, with just enough light from a nearby street-lamp to let me imagine performing my work. In fact, I honestly feel that if some divine power *had* sought to provide the perfect opportunity for me, this is precisely the scene that would be laid out. The woman even stops for a moment, standing unsteadily near the shadows, as if she is waiting for me to go and end her life.

It is at times like this that I almost understand why weaker men believe in God.

The woman starts walking again, and I know now that I must seize my chance.

I set off after her, walking at double her speed as I make my way across the square. I look up at nearby windows, but there is no sign of anybody watching. Ahead, the woman is heading into the shadows, as if she has some instinctive understanding of where I would like her to be when I slit her throat. She seems not to have noticed me at all, and a moment later she stops again. I am tempted to believe that perhaps she knows now that I am here, but in truth she seems to be a drunk wretch and – as I step up behind her and take the knife from my pocket – I realize I can already smell alcohol on her person. Any ordinary woman, in possession of their senses, would have noted my approach already.

Perhaps my earlier failure was a stroke of unexpected luck, if it meant that the mass of idiots and police officers has swarmed toward that yard and away from this particular street.

Suddenly the woman turns, and I take this as my cue to strike.

I hit her hard across the side of the face, causing her to stumble away. Grabbing her by the shoulder, I twist her around and place a hand over her mouth, just in time to keep her from calling out. Then I wrestle her to the ground, easily succumbing her drunken flailing as I adjust my grip and press the knife against her throat. I cannot see her too well in the dark, but I can feel the blade pressing against her neck, so I push and slice. I immediately feel hot blood flowing out across my hand. Her struggles become more violent for a moment, and she tries to bite the palm of my hand, but finally she falls limp in my arms and I lower her down onto the cobbles.

My heart is pounding, but when I look around I see once again that we are completely alone here in this little square. Whereas I was interrupted before, this time I might be able to complete my work.

I roll the woman over, and I'm just about able to make out her dead stare. There is blood all around her mouth, and I suppose I must have caused her to hit her chin on the ground when she fell.

No matter.

Reaching down, I start cutting through her paltry garments until I have exposed her abdomen. And then, after looking one more time to ensure that we are not about to be disturbed, I begin to cut deep into her body so that I might extract the parts I need.

CHAPTER NINE
MADDIE

Today

THE OVERGROWN BUSHES RUSTLE AS I step into the pitch-black garden at the rear of the abandoned house. I can't see anything at all, so it's a surprise when I feel leaves brushing against my face. I hold my hand up to protect myself a little, and to make sure that I don't walk straight into a tree branch, as I fight my way through the undergrowth. This garden is so dark and wild, I feel like I'm forcing my way through a jungle.

Finally, as I feel a set of cracked paving stones beneath my feet, I stop and look up at the rear of the house.

Since there are no street lights around, all I can see now is the vast, dark shape of number nine Cromwell Road silhouetted against the dull orange glow of a London night sky.

Rain is starting to fall heavier and harder than ever, and I can feel my shoulders getting wet. I can't really afford to let my clothes get soaked, so I haul my backpack onto the ground and crouch down. After unzipping the top, I reach inside and fumble for a moment, before finally pulling out the small flashlight I brought when I left home. The two ends have become slightly loose, so it takes a moment for me to screw the thing back together, but eventually I switch the light on and a small but useful beam shines through the rain. At least the battery is holding out for now.

I aim the flashlight toward the house, but all I see are more boarded-up windows.

Getting to my feet, I turn and start looking around. At first I see nothing but overgrown bushes, but finally the beam of light catches the edge of a small wooden building. Struggling to fight my way through the weed-infested garden, I head along what I think used to be a garden path, and after a couple of minutes I reach the shed.

Or rather, the structure that *used* to be the shed.

As more rain falls, I shine the flashlight's beam around and see that the shed's roof has collapsed under the weight of some fallen branches, which have collapsed into the structure and almost entirely demolished one of the walls. I peer closer, but I can already tell that there's no way I'll find any shelter here. Figuring that maybe I could lift part of the broken roof and use it as a basic form of covering, I reach out and try to move the slab of wood, only to find that it's far too heavy. I crouch down and shine the flashlight under, hoping to perhaps find a little hole I can wriggle into, but there's nothing. This was a dead-end and now I'm starting to get really soaked.

"The worst thing is when you get really wet," I remember Alex telling me once. "You can get sick, Maddie. Really sick."

Turning, I look around the garden, double-checking that there's not a second shed. Realizing that there's nowhere to hide out here, I turn and start trudging back through the garden, while trying to think of anywhere else in this part of London where I could maybe go and take cover. I guess there was a bus-stop along the road, and at least I'd be able to stay dry for a few hours, although I'm still jumpy and worried that the guy from the park might show up. Even now, as I shine the flashlight around the overgrown garden, I'm a little nervous in case he's here.

And then, suddenly, the flashlight's beam catches an uncovered half-circle window at the back of the house.

I freeze, convinced that the window must somehow be part of the place next door, but deep down I already know that's not true. As the beam of light blasts through the rain-filled air, I see that a wooden panel appears to have fallen away from one of the windows, and that the latch appears to have been left open. The window itself is partially open, as if long ago somebody thought there was no point fixing it properly, not if a wooden panel was going to be put in place. The glass is broken, and with several large shards still jammed in the frame.

I step closer, until I'm right beneath the window, which is set a little way up in the house's rear wall. Too high to reach easily, but not too far to climb.

"All I know," Alex's voice whispers in my memory, "is that for as long as I've been on the streets, everyone has known to keep away from that house."

I'm sure she's right. I'm sure I should just trust Alex. After all, I've never, *ever* gone against her advice. At the same time, I can't help remembering another thing she told me earlier:

"No-one ever goes in there, no matter how desperate they are. Everyone knows to keep well away. Even the junkies and the addicts don't dare. They feel it too. They feel the utter evil in that house."

If that's true – and Alex never lied – then the house should be completely empty.

One of the dangers of entering a new place, even if it seems abandoned, is that you never know who else might be inside already. After all, I can't be the first person who's noticed this house, or who's come into the garden in search of shelter. In most cases, a house like this would already have squatters in every room, and at best I'd end up trying to haggle for some space on the floor. At worst, I'd find that the people here aren't very nice. But if Alex is right – and she's never been wrong once, not so far – then this house should be completely abandoned. It should be safe, if only for a few hours.

"Can't you feel the evil here?" Alex asked me all those months ago, when we stood out the front of the place. "Can't you feel it reaching out to you?"

My answer now is the same as my answer back

then.

No.

I don't feel any evil at all.

Maybe for once, Alex was wrong. Or if not wrong, then at least... overreacting a little? Besides, she's gone now, so I guess I have to start making my own decisions.

I've got to ignore Alex's advice some day, so why not now? Especially if the alternative is freezing in the rain.

I hesitate for a moment, still trying to think of somewhere else – *anywhere* else – I could go instead. Finally, however, I realize that this is really my best option, so I look around and try to figure out how I'm going to climb up to the window. There aren't a lot of possibilities, but there's a fence I could probably scale, and I'm not too bad at keeping my balance. Deep down, there's a part of me that still thinks this is a really bad idea, but staying out in the open is an even worse possibility so...

Wincing as I feel a flicker of pain in my waist, I haul my backpack off my shoulders and lift it up until it's on the sill at the bottom of the window. I hesitate again, aware that there'll be no going back after this moment, but the truth is that I honestly don't have another option. Finally, therefore, I push my backpack through, and I quickly hear the sound of it hitting the floor inside the house. Some of the shards of glass break, too, but they don't shatter as they land.

And then I start climbing up the fence, taking care not to slip as more and more rain comes crashing down.

CHAPTER TEN
DOCTOR CHARLES GRAZIER

Saturday September 29th, 1888

LIFTING THE KIDNEY FROM THE DEAD WOMAN'S ABDOMEN, I take a moment to reach my knife around to the underside and cut away the final pieces of tissue that are connecting the organ to its host. The blade is a little dull, so I have to slice again and again until finally I feel the tissue tear free. Once that is done, I set the knife aside for a moment and hold the kidney up, so that I might better judge its quality.

The organ is warm and wet with blood, and I believe – despite the poor light – that it is in a decent condition.

I set the kidney on the piece of apron cloth that I prepared, next to the part of the woman's uterus that I managed to remove. Blood is already staining the fabric, and I cannot help but wish that I had come better prepared. Still, as I turn back to look at the woman's open abdomen, I know that I must remain focused on the task at hand. For one thing, I must remove her right kidney as well. For another, I am starting to wonder whether I might take her liver after all. There seems no reason to waste any part of her that might prove useful.

She is a drunk, yes, but the liver seems remarkably well-preserved. In fact, I might be able to -

Suddenly I hear footsteps.

Startled, I turn and look back across the dark square, terrified that I am about to be interrupted. I wait for some sign of a passing police officer, or perhaps another loathesome merchant trader who might indolently wander across my path, but a moment later I realize that the footsteps seem to be leading away again. Still, I know that sooner or later somebody *will* come into the square, so I must finish harvesting this whore's organ's as quickly as possible.

Reaching down, I start digging through her guts again, attempting to find my way to her remaining kidney. In an operating theater, of course, I would have no trouble at all. Matters are a little different out here in the cold, dark night, and I must confess to becoming momentarily lost as my fingers sift through the mass of guts. Finally, however, I locate the second kidney, and I reach for the knife.

Suddenly I hear footsteps again, this time coming from another direction. I freeze for a few seconds, before looking around as I realize that these footsteps seem to be coming closer, echoing all around me in the cold night air. I remain completely silent, hoping against hope that I am not about to be disturbed, but I can already tell that some cursed fool means to enter the square. I want to stay and extract the remaining kidney, but I am already starting to panic and finally – barely even knowing my own actions – I fold the old apron shut and gather the kidney and uterus, before getting to my feet and hurrying along the side of a building. With luck, I shall be able to return in a moment and take the other kidney.

I slip around the corner, and then I stop to listen as the footsteps get closer and closer.

"Alright there!" a man's voice calls out suddenly. "Had a few too many to drink, have we?"

Daring to peer around the corner, I see to my horror that a common beat policeman has walked over to the dead woman and is gently kicking her arm. Evidently he believes her to be a common drunk, although after a moment he crouches down and takes a closer look. Even this idiot must soon realize that the woman is dead.

"What in the name of..."

His voice trails off for a moment.

"No," he says finally, his voice filled with common, pig-ignorant shock, "say it's not so. Please, for the love of..."

Again he falls silent.

And then, scrambling to his feet, he turns and runs.

I watch as the fool hurries across the square, and then finally he stops at the door to a warehouse on the far side. He starts banging on the door, as if he means to raise assistance, and it is quite clear to me now that the dead whore's body has been lost to these do-gooders. Soon enough, the square will be awash with those who believe the life of a whore is something to be protected. Even now, I can hear voices shouting from inside some of the nearby houses, and it is clear enough that I must be out of here before more do-gooders arrive.

With the organs clutched in my arms, wrapped in the whore's apron, I turn and hurry along the street. My escape comes not a moment too soon, as several doors nearby are already being unlocked. Fortunately, however, I am able to reach the next corner before anybody spots me.

Behind me, back in the square, voices are shouting now. It is as if the whole city is suddenly roused by the excitement of a murder, as if a woman might mean nothing when she is alive yet might come to mean a great deal once she is dead. These hypocrites never fail to sicken me, and I am quite sure that the people of this foul city – including my erstwhile former colleague Doctor Thomas Culpepper – will no doubt enjoy reading all the gory details in tomorrow's newspaper. This country has come to a rotten end when crime and murder are treated as a form of entertainment.

I stop again and look down at the bloodied apron, and now I am struck by the realization that perhaps this fabric is causing more harm than good. Unwrapping the apron, I see no obvious signs of damage to either the kidney or the uterus, yet my panic is such that I slide the bloodied masses into my hands and let the apron fall away, before turning and making my way along another street.

I must get home and begin the latest operation immediately. Catherine's life depends upon my haste.

CHAPTER ELEVEN
MADDIE

Today

"DAMN IT!"

Slipping thanks to my wet shoes, I tumble through the window. There's a drop on the other side, and I slam hard against the wooden floor, falling partially on top of my backpack and letting out a gasp of pain. Rolling onto my side, I take a deep breath, only to inhale a load of dust from the air.

I sit up, spluttering and coughing, as I take the flashlight from my pocket and switch it on.

When I shine the beam forward, all I see is a bare, cracked wall with no paper and almost no plaster. I can hear the sound of my own breath in the cold air, and the sound of rain crashing down outside.

I sit in silence for a few minutes, getting my breath back and shining the flashlight around at the walls.

Finally, figuring that I can't stay here on the floor in soaking wet clothes, I start hauling myself up. The hallway floorboards creak as I step forward and grab my backpack. My clothes are drenched, with the fabric of my shirt feeling ice-cold as it clings to my skin. Reaching down, I carefully pull the fabric away from the cut on my waist. When I shine the flashlight down, I see that the material is stained dark red with blood. I'm going to have to find some way to clean that wound soon.

Looking up at the window, I watch the rain for a moment, almost hypnotized by the sight of so much water crashing down from the sky.

After a moment, however, I limp across the room until I reach an open doorway, and then I step out into the hall. Pulling the creaky door shut to quieten the sound of rain, I take a couple more steps forward before stopping in the middle of the hall and turning around, shining the flashlight around and quickly seeing several closed doors as well as a large staircase that rises up through the building and spirals out of view to the right. High above, there's an old chandelier that's hanging slightly askew, and that frankly looks like it might come crashing down at any moment.

From somewhere upstairs, there's the sound of trickling water, almost as if a leak in the roof is allowing some of the storm water to run inside. The air is so cold, I'm actually starting to shiver.

I wait for several minutes, listening for even the slightest hint that somebody else might be here. It's all well and good for me to assume that Alex was right about this place being abandoned, but maybe she was just letting her superstitions run amok. If *I* found that open window, and if *I* was willing to take a chance by coming through, then it's certainly possible that somebody else might be here as well. Still, as the minutes tick past and as I hear only the sound of rain and running water, I can't help but feel that the house certainly *seems* deserted. I guess maybe, for once, I've just been exceptionally lucky.

In fact, not only does there not seem to be anybody here now; I get the feeling this house has been abandoned for a long time.

Finally figuring that I can't just stand here dripping in the dark all night, I start making my way across the hallway. The floorboards creak and buckle slightly beneath my feet, and I feel as if even the slightest noise is somehow an intrusion, as if I'm disturbing the peace of a house that has been left alone for so very long. I almost want to mutter an apology, but I manage to keep my mouth shut as I reach out and fumble for the cold metal handle on the door next to the stairs.

My heart is pounding, but I force myself to turn the handle and push the door open. Sure enough, and as I expected, the hinges creak, and when I shine the flashlight through I see a fairly large, empty room with no furniture. There's a large, open fireplace on the far side, but when I look at the windows I see only some broken glass panes and – on the other side – the backs of the wooden boards. I think I'm at the front of the house, so this is one of the rooms overlooking the front garden and the street. It's not particularly welcoming in here, but I guess all the rooms are going to be more or less the same, so I step inside and drop my backpack onto the floor before crouching down and starting to sort through my few possessions.

It takes a moment before I find the blanket I brought from home. As I pull the blanket out and unfold it, I feel the fabric to check that it's dry. Fortunately the backpack is water-proof, and the lining has held up, so I get to my feet and start stripping out of my soaking wet clothes. In a place like this, they'll take a while to dry, but hopefully they'll at least be a little better by morning.

I certainly can't afford to get sick.

At that moment, as if to warn me, I sneeze.

Once I'm out of the clothes, I look around for somewhere to hang them. There aren't many options, so finally I arrange them over the backs of chairs that I set around the old fireplace. I wrap the blanket around my shivering shoulders, and almost immediately I feel a little better.

"Never go into that house, Maddie," I hear Alex's voice whispering in my head.

What else was I supposed to do?

Even Alex can't be right *every* time.

It's dumb, but this blanket around my shoulders is the blanket from my bed. I've had this blanket since I was a kid, and somehow it always makes me feel safer. Not that I *am* safer, of course, but even the slightest sense of comfort is welcome right now as I stand in an abandoned house, with no dry clothes, shivering with a meager flashlight between my teeth. I remember my mother settling the blanket over my bed before kissing me goodnight when I was a little girl, and I remember my grandmother reminding me to pack it in my suitcase when I moved house. After living on the streets for almost a year now, I've pretty much hit rock-bottom, but this blanket somehow keeps me feeling as if I've still got hope.

As if I'm still *me*.

I remember the night I ran away from home. I remember shoving stuff into my backpack, trying to make sure that I only took things I'd really need. The blanket seemed like too much at the time – too heavy and too bulky, and way too sentimental – and I almost left it out, but then I realized that maybe I'd need to keep warm. In the end I left several pairs of jeans behind, and some shirts too, solely because I thought the blanket might be useful. And sure enough, after a couple more minutes, I realize that I'm no longer shivering.

I won't be alone and homeless forever. One day I'll have my own place, and this blanket is the one thing I've kept from my old life. The one thing I plan to keep forever.

Taking the flashlight in my right hand, I look down at my waist. I can't see around to the back, so I can't see the wound from the knife, but I'm starting to think that I must have been extraordinarily lucky. I'm in pain, and there's definitely blood, but I actually feel reasonably alert now, as if the initial shock has subsided. I reach behind and touch the wound and I feel fresh blood, but somehow I'm still on my feet. I always figured a stab wound would pretty much knock me off my feet, but I guess the blade must have missed all my vital organs. If this had been a serious injury, there's no way I'd have been able to run, let alone still be standing right now.

Either that, or I actually died back there in the park and everything since has been a dying fever dream. Then again, I don't think I'd feel so cold in a dream.

I desperately want to sleep, and my eyes will definitely close if I sit down, but I know that'd be dangerous while I'm so cold. I have to keep my mind busy while I wait for morning. I shuffle back out into the hallway before stopping to lean against the wall. I'm shivering again, and I reach down to my waist yet again, hoping to find that at least the wound has finally stopped bleeding.

Instead, I feel fresh blood dribbling from the torn flesh.

Or is that just old blood, mixed with sweat or rain water?

It'll heal.

It has to heal.

If it doesn't heal...

No.

I'm not going to think about what might happen if it doesn't heal.

Alex would know what to do right now, but I have to stop thinking like that. Alex is gone, she split and left me, and I probably won't even see her again. I have no right to be angry, but at the same time I can't carry her around in my head like some voice of wisdom.

Alex was my best friend for a while, and she sure saved me on a few occasions, but she's gone now and I can manage without her.

I'm alone now.

I can handle being alone.

There's nothing *wrong* with being alone. Nothing at all.

Suddenly I hear a clicking sound over my shoulder, followed by the start of a slow, groaning creak.

Spinning around and holding the flashlight up, I see that a door in the far corner is slowly swinging open. The creaking sound continues until finally the door bumps against the wall, revealing a pitch-black space.

I stay completely still, watching the open doorway. I know full well that the door must have opened because of a breeze, or that maybe by being here I accidentally disturbed the pressure or something, but it's still a little creepy. I'm worried that someone might suddenly come running through, but the house seems completely silent and after several minutes I feel brave enough to start shuffling over to the doorway.

Don't get jumpy.

I run those three words through my head over and over, trying to make myself take them to heart. Trying to believe them.

When I get to the far side of the hall, I take hold of the door and try swinging it shut. Sure enough, there's the same creaking sound, and I quickly see that there's a slightly loose latch that's supposed to keep the door closed. I shut the door and put the latch in place, and then I give the door a wiggle. Sure enough, the latch barely holds, and as I pull the door open again I realize that it probably wouldn't take much for the whole thing to come loose. Letting go of the door, I find that it seems to naturally open all the way, until once again it bumps against the wall.

And then, as if to add another point, there's a rumble of thunder in the distance and I hear the glass rattling in a nearby window.

If this storm was much louder and stronger, maybe the whole house would shake apart. I've been out in storms like this before. Not often, but often enough to know that they can really cause some serious damage. In fact, it's a miracle that an old place like this is still standing at all.

I turn to head back over to my sleeping bag, but then I stop and look down the wooden steps that lead into the basement. The last thing I want is to go and take a look right now, but I can't quite bring myself to step back and swing the door shut. The whole house seems so cold, but somehow the air here at the top of the steps seems warmer, and when I reach my hand out I find that I stop shivering almost immediately. Holding my flashlight up, I shine the beam down the steps, and a scene that should be cold and uninviting instead feels like the only logical place to go.

Besides, if I go to my sleeping bag, or even if I just sit down, I might fall asleep. And in my current state, falling asleep might just be lethal.

I have to stay awake, and on my feet, and focused on something.

So that's why, after checking that the wooden

steps feel safe, I start cautiously making my way down into the basement.

CHAPTER TWELVE
DOCTOR CHARLES GRAZIER

Saturday September 29th, 1888

STANDING IN THE HALLWAY, beneath the grand chandelier, I realize that I am delaying for no good reason. I look toward the stairs, and I know in my heart that the time has come for the next procedure. I can only hope that Catherine will understand, and that she will not resist.

***

"No!" she screams, delirious with rage and fear as I try to lift her from the bed. "Charles, stop! Charles, I can't bear this again!"

Ignoring her cries, I take hold of her frail wrists and twist her around. She kicks furiously, as if she means to force me away, but I am wise to her tactics. I shift around to the bottom of the bed and pull hard, dragging Catherine across the crumpled sheets until she lands in the wheelchair that I brought up, and then I quickly slip her right hand into one of the manacles that I hate so much.

She starts trying to pull the hand free, which gives me a chance to get around her and grab her other hand, forcing this too into a tight bind that will keep her from escaping.

Only in a godless world would a good man have to tie his wife down in such a way.

"Charles, I'm begging you!" she sobs, shaking with such force that the chair's metal frame almost topples over. "No more! Please, have mercy and just let me die!"

"Catherine -"

"No, listen to me!" she continues, her voice filled with panic. "Let me die, Charles, so that I shall no longer have to suffer in this manner. Let me die and slip the pain, else I think I shall be driven mad. I cannot face being cut open and re-stitched, not again. This is no way to live. I would rather die!"

And only in a godless world would a good man have to hear his darling wife say such things.

"You are sick, my dear," I reply, grabbing the handles and pulling the chair back before starting to wheel Catherine toward the door. "Your blood is poisoned. You do not know what you're saying and this insensible -"

"Please, Charles!" she whimpers. "Don't make me do this! Don't do this *to* me! I can't take the pain a moment longer..."

Just as I am about to tell her again to calm down, she tries again to tear herself from the chair. She fails, of course, but in the process she bumps me and causes one of the chair's handles to smash my hand against the doorjamb. I let out a gasp of pain and pull away, and when I look down I see a bloodied graze at the base of my thumb. There is clearly no greater damage, but I am shocked by the violence of my wife's anger. It is as if she truly does not understand that I am only trying to help her.

If I were a lesser man, no doubt I would worry that she had been possessed by some demonic force.

"Catherine," I say firmly, stepping around the constantly-shaking chair and seeing the abject fury in her face as she continues to struggle. "This is most unlike you. You must -"

"Kill me!" she screams, trying to lunge at me but succeeding only in tightening the manacles around her wrists. She is red-faced and frantic, however, and the vein on her forehead is more prominent than ever. "If you ever loved me, Charles, you would kill me now! Do not force me to endure another of your monstrous experiments!"

"It is an *operation*," I remind her, "a procedure designed to save your -"

"Kill me!"

"Catherine -"

"KILL ME!"

"I would sooner die myself than lose you!" I shout, momentarily losing my senses. Breathless now, I take a step toward her, and I can see the shock in her eyes. "I cannot live without you," I stammer. "I can save you. I have made mistakes before, but this time I am certain of the procedure."

"You said that before!" she sobs.

"But this time -"

"And before that," she continues, as tears stream down her face, "and before that too. There is nothing you can do, Charles, but let me go in peace. Without pain."

I shake my head.

"How many procedures is it now?" she asks.

"Catherine..."

"This will be the sixth, will it not?"

I pause, before nodding.

"Each one more painful than the last," she continues. "Each one leaving me more wrecked than before. The cancer is part of me now, Charles. Whatever you do, whatever you take out of me and replace, the cancer will grow back. You're like Canute, fighting a losing battle. And each time you fight, the pain becomes so much worse."

I open my mouth to tell her that this time will be different, but for a moment the words catch in my throat. I understand that I might sound as if I am repeating myself, but there is no time to explain why time time will be different.

"Please," she adds, and now she turns her right hand so that I might see the palm, as if she expects me to take her hand in mine. "You are a brilliant surgeon, Charles," she whimpers, her voice trembling so much that I can barely make out any of the words, "almost certainly the greatest of your generation, but you cannot save me. Nobody can. You are only prolonging the agony for both of us."

"I *can* save you," I reply, although now my voice too is shaking. "I *can*, Catherine. I just need to complete this one final procedure and -"

"Where do you get them from, Charles?"

I feel a shudder pass through my chest. "I beg your pardon?"

"Where do you get the things you put into me?" she continues, and now she is eyeing me with a note of cold suspicion. "Sometimes I wake at night and you are not in the house."

"Of course I'm in the -"

"No, you're not," she adds, shaking her head. "Where do you go until two or three some mornings?"

"I -"

"Always the mornings before you try a new procedure on me."

I shake my head, although I know she is right.

"Don't lie to me, Charles. I have always, *always* known when you're lying." She pauses, watching me with a growing sense of concern. "Do I want to know, Charles? Do I want to know the truth about where you go, or about how you acquire the things you sew into my innards? You don't get them from any of the colleges, I know that. They'd never give you such items. And you don't get them from the hospitals or from your colleagues. So where *do* you get them from? And why when you come home do you always have that look in your eyes?"

"What look?" I ask.

She watches me carefully, as if she is searching for something in my eyes.

"There is no look in my eyes," I stammer. "You are imagining things in your fever."

"*That* look," she replies. "A look of guilt. Do not even think to deny it, for I see it even now. Oh Charles, you are a good man and I love you. Please, end this horror and just let me die."

She tries to reach toward me, to take my hands, but her wrists merely strain against the manacles and cause the chains to clink against the sides of the chair.

"Death is not the most awful things that can happen to a soul, you know," she continues. "You do these things for the right reasons, but please, when I die... Let me see not guilt in your eyes, but acceptance and peace. That is all I ask. I want you to still be yourself when my end comes, not twisted by desperation into some kind of monster."

I wait for her to continue, but I think perhaps that she in turn is waiting for me to bow down to her will. Her tears have stopped, although her cheeks still glisten, and it is abundantly clear that she thinks she has changed my mind.

Out in the street, a crude ruffian shouts at the top of his voice.

Still Catherine stares at me.

We are wasting time here.

"This one operation will solve everything," I say finally, "and -"

"Oh no," she sobs, lowering her gaze to her lap as if she has finally given up. "No, Charles, no..."

"This one operation will save you," I continue, reaching down and placing a hand on the side of her sweaty, bowed face. There are tears in *my* eyes now.

"Charles, please..."

"Catherine..."

"Lord have mercy," she continues, and suddenly I realize she is speaking not to me, but to some higher power. My wife – my calm, rational-minded wife, has turned in her hour of need to the one thing she always swore to disavow.

She has turned to God.

I feel rather disgusted.

"Take me into your arms, Lord," she sobs. "Help me leave this ruined body."

"Catherine," I say firmly, "you are not in your right mind. You must abandon these feeble ideas at once."

"Please, Lord," she whispers. "Mercy, I beg of you..."

"I promise, Catherine," I continue, "that I have learned the lessons of past failures. I have planned tonight's procedure extensively, and this time I -"

Suddenly she starts sobbing louder than ever. Huge, convulsive sobs that cause her entire body to shake, and that leave tears dripping down onto the creased fabric of her nightshirt.

"I have learned the lessons of past failures," I tell her again, "and I am certain, beyond all doubt, that this time I shall free you from the shackles of your illness. This time the cancer will be gone, and it shall not have a chance to come back. The operation will take a few hours, and then your recovery can begin, and then within a few weeks my darling you shall be back on your feet and this will all feel like a bad dream. Why, we can even go traveling, perhaps to -"

She lets out a sudden wailing sound, as if she has taken leave of her senses.

"Just have faith in me," I continue. "Do that, and I shall not let you down. Not this time."

I wait for her to respond, but she simply continues to sob. Finally I step back around the chair and start wheeling her toward the stairs, so that I might bump her down to the basement. She seems utterly bereft of hope, yet I know that this time the operation will be a success, that this time I have found a way to end Catherine's suffering and to return her to full health. At least she has accepted that the procedure must go ahead. Now it is my job to prove to her that I can save her from her illness.

"There there," I say as I wheel her along the corridor, and as she continues to sob, "everything will be alright this time. I promise. I shall begin the procedure as soon as I get you down to the basement."

CHAPTER THIRTEEN
MADDIE

Today

THIS PLACE IS HUGE.

Standing at the foot of the wooden stairs, I aim the flashlight around and see that the basement is a vast, open space with stone walls that rise up to join in a high ceiling. There are several thick pillars that look like they've been reinforced to support the weight of the house, and each pillar seems slightly buckled, almost as if the house is too heavy and could come crashing down at any moment.

Stepping forward, I see that there's some kind of table in the center of the room. As I get closer, however, I see that my flashlight's beam is in fact falling not on a table but on a kind of large stone slab with deep lines carved into its surface. As I get to the side of the slab, I reach down and place a hand on the cold stone, feeling the rough surface and dipping my hands into one of the grooves. Looking along to the table's far end, I see that the grooves all meet at the base, almost as if they're designed to channel liquid away from the slab's surface. And as I tilt the flashlight a little, I realize that the grooves seem darker than the rest of the stone, almost as if they were stained long ago.

I take a step back, and in the process my right foot bumps against a ridge on the ground. Aiming the flashlight down, I find that just as there's a pattern of ridges on the slab, there are more ridges in a similar pattern on the ground, leading to a series of what look like drains set into the corners of the room. It's almost as if the whole room was designed to funnel blood down from the table and then over to the drains. With the flashlight still raised, I start slowly turning to look all around, and I'm starting to think that some crazy stuff went down in this place. Then again, I'm probably letting my imagination run a little wild.

And then I spot the tables nearby.

Making my way over, I shine the flashlight at the tabletops and see what looks like a set of tools. When I examine them more closely, I realize that there are old knives and scalpels, and various other items that seem to be the rusty remains of a surgeon's kit. I pick up one of the scalpels and find that the handle is old and slightly loose, although the blade shines clean in the flashlight's beam. I can't even begin to imagine what all this stuff would once have been used for, but it's pretty clear from the layer of dust that none of the items have been used for years. I guess maybe a doctor used to live here, and...

A cold shiver runs through my chest as I turn and look back over at the stone table.

Blood.

Maybe I was right first time. The dark stains in the grooves *must* be blood, as if some long-gone psycho used this place as an operating theater. In fact, as I shine the flashlight all around, I realize that I'm probably bang on the money. Whatever happened here in the past, it must have been some kind of at-home surgical set-up. I have no idea whether stuff like that was illegal in the old days, or even uncommon, but the thought is enough to make me feel seriously uncomfortable. Even if this was a legitimate old-time operating theater, I really don't like the idea of being down here. I bet the standards weren't too high back then. I bet people were in real agony.

Turning, I start heading back toward the door. I know I'll be colder up in the main part of the house, but at least I won't be freaked out. I can -

Tap!

Tap!

Tap!

I freeze as soon as I hear them. For a moment I tell myself that the three tapping sounds were all in my head, but I quickly realize that this isn't true. I turn and shine my flashlight back across the basement, but now everything is silent again. For a moment, staying completely still, I can't help worrying that maybe somebody is hiding behind one of those stone pillars. There's room for a person to stand out of sight, although the entire basement is deathly quiet and I can't help thinking that I'd be able to hear someone breathing.

I step to one side, turning the flashlight slightly, but I still don't see anyone.

I feel my blood start to run a little cold, before I take a deep breath and force myself to keep my senses straight. I definitely heard three very clear, very abrupt tapping sounds, but in a house this old – and with a heavy thunderstorm still raging outside – it's not difficult to believe that the house itself is simply settling a little. Either that, or maybe a stray rat bumped against one of the stone pillars. In fact, it'd be a miracle if a place like this *didn't* have rats. Everywhere in London has rats.

"Keep it together," I whisper to myself, determined to hold onto what little sanity I have left. "This'd be a really bad time to go loopy."

I wait, but now all I hear is the sound of the storm raging outside the house.

After a moment, I turn and head back over toward the steps. This time, I -

Tap!

Tap!

Tap!

I turn quickly, aiming the flashlight toward the wall, and now I know without a shadow of a doubt that I heard something.

The sound was exactly the same as before: three quick taps, as if something is trying to get my attention, and this time I feel as if the sound came from over near the stone slab. Or if not the slab, then the tools on the nearby tables. I shine the beam toward the medical instruments, waiting – and hoping – to see a rat scurry past.

I wait, but no rat appears.

My hand is trembling, causing the flashlight's beam to shake wildly.

As the seconds tick past, however, I start to realize that I'm letting myself get carried away, and that I really need to get a grip before I spiral into some kind of paranoia.

This is how people lose their minds.

"There's nothing here," I whisper, and somehow those words seem to calm me a little.

There's nothing here.

If the sound wasn't caused by a rat, then maybe it was caused by water. Yeah, that makes sense. There's rain outside, and a dribble of water is somehow getting down into the basement and hitting the floor. I mean, I *think* that makes sense. Right now, it'll do as an explanation.

I pause, listening to the sound of the storm, and then I turn to walk back to the stairs. With each step, I expect to hear a sudden tapping sound coming once again from over my shoulder, but as I get to the door I feel a flicker of relief as I realize that this time there seems to be nothing. In fact, as I start making my way up the stairs, I actually start wondering whether -

Tap!

It's in my head.

Tap!

Tap!

I flinch as I feel the sound echoing through my skull. I feel the pressure, too, and I quickly drop down to my knees. The sound has already ended, but as I slowly turn and look back across the basement, I feel a flash of fear.

The tapping wasn't at the tables this time.

It was in my head.

I felt something tapping three times on the inside of my skull, scraping against the bone.

I wait, watching the basement with a growing sense of dread. If something over there wanted to get my attention, it certainly succeeded. All I want right now is to turn around and run up the wooden stairs, and then seal the door shut and run far away. At the same time, I feel as if I have to confront my fear, and finally – almost without realizing what I'm doing – I start shuffling back across the basement, heading past the stone slab and over toward the tables.

If I run, I'll always wonder what just happened.

I'll always have doubts.

Instead, I'm going to figure this out.

Suddenly I feel something wet on my left foot. I stop and shine the flashlight down, and to my horror I see that blood has washed down from the wound on my waist, covering my leg and foot. I reach down and touch the wound, and at that moment I feel a sudden rush of weakness. I take a step back, but my head is spinning slightly and I startle myself by bumping against one of the stone pillars. Glad of the support, I lean against the stone and try to find the strength to start walking again, but now my knees feel weak and I'm worried I might be about to collapse.

I touch the wound again.

Am I imagining things, or are the edges slightly

swollen now?

Finally I let myself slide down onto my knees, and I feel a sense of panic starting to grip my chest. Turning, I look back across the basement and see that I've left a trail of bloodied footprints criss-crossing the basement.

And then I close my eyes, and the last thing I feel is my body slamming down against the cold stone floor.

CHAPTER FOURTEEN
DOCTOR CHARLES GRAZIER

Saturday September 29th, 1888

MY HANDS ARE SHAKING.

Why are my hands shaking?

Again, my body betrays me. Again, when I need steadiness, my hands shake as if they are the hands of a common beggar. I operated on so many people during my career and I never experienced so much as a tremor. Why, then, do my hands betray me now?

"Control yourself, man," I whisper under my breath. "Get a grip."

Outside, a thunder storm has begun to rumble in the sky, and rain is beating down.

Frustrated, I turn and look back across the room. Catherine is still on the table, still unconscious after the injection I gave her, and I should already have begun the procedure. Even now, the kidney waits in its metal pan, most likely degrading with each passing second that I waste. It is of the utmost importance that I begin the operation immediately, yet I know that I cannot do any work until my hands are under control.

If I were a praying man, I suppose I would be on my knees.

Fortunately, I am a man of science, so I need not rely on such ephemeral things. I have other ways to steady myself.

Looking down at my hands again, I stare at the weak, pathetic, trembling things and I tell myself that through sheer willpower alone I can bring my body under control. I am Doctor Charles Grazier, one of the most esteemed surgeons in all of London, and my mind is stronger than my body. The flesh shall not run ramshackle over this moment, and I shall impose my mind's will upon my meat and bones. Other men may lack this ability, but I refuse to be beaten. My body is going to obey my mind.

Catherine needs me to be strong. And it is for her sake that I shall be strong.

***

With steady hands, I lower the still-warm kidney into Catherine's open abdomen and settle it gently into its new home. As I slip my fingers away, the kidney remains firmly in place, and I can already see that it fits rather well.

"Do not fear," I whisper, glancing at my dear wife's face and seeing that her eyes are still closed.

"Everything is going according to plan. I shall not let you down."

Still, I cannot help but glance down at the stone floor. Catherine has lost a little more blood than I had anticipated, and now the blood has run from the table and is trickling along toward one of the drains in the far wall. I should like to collect my darling wife's blood, but I have no time for that now.

I cannot be sentimental.

Instead, I turn back to the task at hand. Taking hold of the kidney's upper end, I start searching for the material that I shall sew directly into Catherine's body. I have undertaken extensive study of the human kidney, to the extent that I dare say I know the organ better than any man alive. I understand every aspect of its structure, and it takes me only a moment to find the thick, fibrous tube that I must stitch tight to the opening in Catherine's own body.

I reach for a bottle of alcohol and pour half its contents over the kidney. This is the part of the procedure that I omitted last time, the part that will surely cleanse the organ and guarantee that it takes root on this occasion. After all, once the alien bacteria from the whore's body have been destroyed, bacteria from Catherine's body will be able to populate the kidney and bind it more securely to its new home. This, I am certain, is the final part of the puzzle, the part that will make the operation a success.

Soon, her pain will be ended.

Suddenly hearing a faint murmur, I look over at Catherine's face. Her lips are twitching, but her eyes are still shut and I quickly tell myself that there is no cause for concern. She is not about to cry out in pain, nor shall she leap from the table and try to run. She is unconscious and she will *remain* unconscious for as long as I need her to stay on this table. And later, when she wakes and feels that her health has returned, she will thank me. Not that I require her thanks, of course. All I require is her survival, and her presence by my side.

I reach over and take a threaded needle from the bench.

And then I wait.

I should be sewing the kidney into Catherine's body now, yet for some reason I find myself hesitating. Deep down, I feel a flicker of doubt, as if some part of me worries that the operation will not succeed. This is nonsense, of course, yet I can almost feel tiny threads on the insides of my arms, trying to pull me back. Catherine is at peace now, and it would be the work of a moment to give her one final injection that would end her suffering forever. For a brief moment, I actually catch myself contemplating the impossible.

I could set her free.

And then I would be without her.

I close my eyes for a moment, already feeling the presence of tears. In my heart, I know that Catherine's death would mean my own as well. I could no more live without my dear wife than I could live without my own blood. She is the best part of me, and in the wake of her passing I would surely have no option but to follow her. A world without Catherine is a world I cannot contemplate, a world I cannot even imagine, a world filled with absolutely nothing but the swollen ache of sorrow. At the same time, if I have any doubt in my ability to save her, I must surely be merciful and let her slip away in peace.

No, I shall save her.

We shall be happy again.

I can do this.

Opening my eyes, I reach into her abdomen and begin to search for the point at which I shall begin sewing. I take a moment to wipe away some more blood, and then I set to work. There is still *much* blood, of course, which makes the job rather difficult and slippery. Still, I am able to sew with delicacy and with firm hands, and the task takes a surprisingly short amount of time. After a mere ten minutes or so, I have completed the main part of the procedure, and the whore's kidney is now a part of my wife's body. In fact, as I set the needle and thread aside, I cannot help but note that the kidney looks as if it *belongs* in its new home. This time, the operation is going to succeed, and I have no doubt about that fact.

Yet there is blood.

So much blood, more blood than usual, more blood than I had anticipated.

So much, in fact, that I can hear it trickling down the drain.

Indeed, the more I sew, the more blood comes flooding out, both from the kidney and from Catherine's own body. I take a scalpel and try to move some of the flesh aside, hoping to find the source of the flow, but in truth the blood seems to be coming from everywhere all at once. A moment later I hear a faint moan emerge from Catherine's lips, but when I look at her face I see that she is still unconscious. Still, something seems to be going wrong, so I set the scalpel aside and rush to the counter, from which I take some cotton padding and a set of clamps. If Catherine loses too much more blood, she will be in great danger.

For the next few minutes, I work furiously.

Every time I stop one source of blood, another seems to open, flooding Catherine's abdomen. It is as if her body is determined to lose more and more at any cost, as if her flesh is fighting back against my attempts to save my dear wife. I can only assume that just as *my* hands sought to betray *me*, so too does her body seek in its own way to betray her desire to survive. My hands are covered in blood now, so much so that the clamps slip whenever I try to grip them, but I manage to keep working until finally, by some miracle, the flow of blood seems to slow.

I work on, determined to counter every last drop. Eventually I begin to feel as if I have won, although a moment later I spot another tell-tale dribble emerging from between the thick black wire that I have used for stitching. I wipe the blood away, but more comes soon enough and I realize with a growing sense of horror that the stitches have begun to come loose.

I reach for the needle again, and then I look back at the kidney just in time to see more and more blood erupting from the wound. Even as I try once again to stem the tide, it is as if Catherine's body is once again doing its best to thwart my every move.

There is blood everywhere. The kidney is coming loose and Catherine is already beginning to look pale.

"No!" I gasp as I work faster and faster, trying to stop the flow of blood even as more coming flooding into her abdomen. "I won't let this happen! I refuse!"

CHAPTER FIFTEEN
MADDIE

Today

THE PAIN WAKES ME SUDDENLY, but when I open my eyes I see only darkness.

Gasping, I realize I can feel something digging into my waist. I reach down and immediately feel my fingers brushing against some kind of thick black wire. I have no idea what's happening, but I think I'm flat on my back and resting on the stone floor.

I try to sit up, but an excruciating pain rips through my waist and I let out a brief whimper as I settle back down. My hands are still shaking and my fingers are getting wrapped deep in the wire, causing the wire's loops to tug at the wound, and my fingers are wet and sticky with blood. I try to pull my hands away, and finally I'm able to disentangle the fingers of my right hand from all the wire. I still can't see anything, although when I turn to the left I spot my flashlight over on the floor, but somehow further down, almost as if...

I hesitate for a moment, before reaching down and feeling the stones beneath me. Even before I feel the deep, blood-filled grooves, I know that I'm not on the floor at all. I'm on the stone slab in the center of the basement and -

Suddenly a hand clamps tight over my mouth, pushing down hard as I try to scream.

CHAPTER SIXTEEN
DOCTOR CHARLES GRAZIER

Sunday September 30th, 1888

FINALLY, ALL IS STILL.

All is quiet.

She has stopped bleeding and I am done.

She lost a great deal of blood, but not so much that she will die. She will be weak for some time, I'm quite sure, but she has a strong constitution and I am certain she can still make a full recovery. So long as she bleeds no more, I believe that her inate strength will pull her through. Catherine has always had a kind of steel in her heart, a determination to keep on living. It is this spirit that makes her so strong, and I know she will pull through.

I believe in her.

It is time now to sew her belly up and set her on the path to recovery. First, though, I take one final quick look at my night's work, just so that I can be sure I have left no loose ends. Spotting a small section of tubing that is poking out from the side of the stitching, I realize that I should make my work as neat as possible. I reach for the scalpel, only to find that it no longer rests on the edge of the table.

I look around, but the scalpel is indeed gone.

I know without a shadow of doubt that I set the instrument down on the table's edge, and I am certain I would have heard if I had knocked it to the floor. Still, I look down at the stones beneath the table, before looking back at the spot where the scalpel should be resting. All I see, however, is Catherine's hand. Of the scalpel, there is no sign whatsoever.

I must have misremembered.

Supposing myself to have made a simple error, I turn and head over to the counter where I keep my tools. It is late, and I am exhausted, and the misplacement of one little scalpel is not, I tell myself, any great disaster. Even the most brilliant men must surely have an occasional lapse. Still, as I search for this particular scalpel among the others, I find to my consternation that it is still missing. Evidently I did not set it here, as I had assumed, which means it must still be over at the table. There is simply nowhere else for it to be.

Yet it is not there.

I spend several minutes searching, determined to find where I left the missing implement, but it seems to have vanished entirely. I grow increasingly frustrated, reminding myself over and over again that I am not the kind of man who loses things. Indeed, I do not remember ever losing a single item during my entire career, since I always have the presence of mind to conduct my work with care. I have always taken great pride in my sense of order.

But this scalpel, this cursed little piece of metal that is barely five inches long, is entirely gone.

As I continue to search, I begin to feel as if I am losing my mind. There is nowhere else in this entire room, nowhere for the scalpel to have fallen or slipped away. I even check at the foot of the wooden stairs, just in case in some moment of panic I kicked the scalpel and sent it skittering across the floor, yet there is still nothing to be found. The scalpel is a solid object, and solid objects do not simply disappear, but no amount of logic seems sufficient to actually help me find what I am looking for. It is almost as if the scalpel somehow slipped out of existence.

Finally, exhausted, I stop at the foot of the table and lean against my hands, trying to get my breath back and – more importantly – to organize my mind.

I shall find the scalpel eventually.

It is here, and it will turn up later.

I do not need to prove such things to myself now.

I must reluctantly admit that it takes several minutes before I am able to cast doubt and superstition from my mind, but ultimately I succeed in reasoning with myself. I shall waste no more time on this fruitless hunt. I know the scalpel is here, so I do not need to prove this fact. I'm quite certain that I shall come down later and locate it with ease.

Stepping around to the other end of the table, I reach down and brush away matted hair from the sides of Catherine's face. She is caked in sweat but still unconscious, and as I look at her beautiful features I cannot help but feel a flickering sense of hope in my chest. I still have to sew her belly shut, of course, but I am certain that her body has already begun to heal itself, and that soon I shall be able to see the first proper signs of her improvement. Even now, the new kidney will be introducing itself to the rest of her body and preparing to take on all the normal functions of such an organ. I know with absolute certainty that I have made no mistakes.

This time in a year, Catherine will be laughing and dancing, and I am sure it will seem silly to ever think back to this awful moment.

"I have saved you," I whisper, still stroking her hair. "Your pain and suffering will soon be over. You will be better than ever."

I wait, almost as if I expect her to answer me, but of course she cannot. The solutions in her bloodstream will keep her unconscious for many hours to come, and I shall top them up as necessary. Given the extent of the surgery I have performed tonight, it might be wise to keep Catherine fully sedated for a couple of days, so that there's no risk of her waking and feeling any pain. As I stroke her hair a little more and stare down at her beautiful face, I feel utterly horrified by the idea that my poor darling might *ever* experience another moment of discomfort. Not after she has already been through so much. I must save her from all of that, as I have saved her from death.

Finally, I step around the table and take the thick black wire, and then I set to work sewing her belly shut. I take such absolute care, threading each loop of wire with calm precision. There will be scarring, of course, but my dear Catherine will undoubtedly continue to grow more beautiful with each passing day. She now has her whole life ahead of her, and our future has been saved.

We faced death together, and we pushed its foul hands from our shoulders. Now the darkness can start to lift from our lives.

CHAPTER SEVENTEEN
MADDIE

Today

THE STORM HAS STOPPED.

That's the first thought that springs into my mind as my eyes flicker open. And then, as I try to remember where I am and how I got here, I see a door in the distance with a faint trace of morning light coming from the top of a set of wooden stairs. For a moment – one stupid moment – I actually wonder whether I'm back at home in my old room, before the truth leaks into my thoughts and I realize the truth.

I remember those stairs.

I remember -

Suddenly I take a deep breath, and I let out an immediate cry of pain as I feel something sharp tugging at my waist. I try to sit up, but now the pain is throbbing and in a panic I try to look down. There's very little light in here, but as I frantically pull the blanket open I see to my horror that not only is there blood all over the fabric, but also the bare skin around my waist is caked in thick patches of blood that looks to have dried in a set of smears. And at the heart of all the blood, there are several loops of what looks like thick black wire poking out from my skin.

***

Letting out another cry as I reach the top of the stairs, I lean against the jamb and stop to look down once more at my waist.

There's just enough light up here for me to be able to see the mess of stitched loops that are keeping my wound closed. There's nothing neat about what's been done to me. Quite the opposite, in fact: the stitches are haphazard and irregular, and in several places it looks as if the wire has been crossed over the same point more than once, as if the wound wasn't quite sealing properly. Some parts of the wire are poking out by almost an inch in thick loops, and one end hasn't even been cut off, instead left dangling so that it hangs down and brushes against my knee.

But the wound has been sealed, and I'm not bleeding anymore.

I remember waking up at one point and feeling pain in my side, and there was also the sensation of a hand over my mouth. I have no idea exactly what happened, but – as I back against the wall and look across the hallway – I can't deny that one thing is very obvious. During the night, somebody stitched my wound back together and stopped the bleeding, which means I'm not alone in the house.

There are even semi-fingerprints in the dried blood around the wound.

Trying not to panic, I wait for a moment before turning and hurrying through to the front room. I quickly find my clothes and pick them up, only to find that they're still soaking wet from the thunderstorm. I start trying to wring some water out of my shirt, but the fabric's heavy and I know I'm on a hiding to nothing. Still, the sense of panic is rising and I feel like I have to get out of this house as fast as possible, before anyone comes back and finds me. I toss the shirt aside and pick up my trousers, but these too are still soaking wet. Finally giving up on trying to dry them, I reach down and start slipping my left leg into the trousers, so that -

Suddenly I hear a bell ringing somewhere in the house.

The sound startles me so much, I start to spin around, only to lose my footing and crash down against the dusty floor. Then I sit in terrified silence, listening to the sound of the empty house.

It was a brief sound, already over by the time I fell, but I know without a shadow of doubt that it was real.

I heard a bell ringing somewhere inside this house.

My left foot is still inside the sopping wet trouser leg, but after a moment I lift the foot out an set my trousers aside.

There's somebody in this house with me, but I'm starting to realize that maybe I shouldn't panic. After all, if this person wanted to hurt me, they had ample opportunity during the night. I was unconscious for several hours. I could have been tortured, raped, murdered or hacked to pieces, or maybe even all those things. I could have been tied up or imprisoned in the basement, but none of that happened.

Instead, I was lifted onto the stone table and then my wound was stitched. Those aren't the actions of a monster. They're the actions of somebody who wants to help. I guess this house wasn't abandoned after all, but whoever's here – whoever helped me – they don't seem to be dangerous.

I wait a moment longer, before pulling the blanket tight as I get to my feet and limp back to the door.

When I lean out into the hallway, I see that the door to the basement is still open, while the house's main staircase winds up high to the upper floors, past a boarded-shut window that lets in just a frame of light around its edges. The chandelier is hanging high above, still slightly skewed and still looking as if it might fall at any moment.

I listen for a few seconds, but my mysterious savior – whoever he or she might be – isn't making a sound now.

My lips tremble, and I can't quite decide whether it would be wise or stupid to speak. I can definitely imagine Alex telling me to run as fast as I can, but then again maybe Alex wasn't always right about things.

Finally, I figure that the person here in the house obviously made an effort to help me. I should at least try to thank him. Or her.

"Hello?" I call out, and I'm immediately shocked by how small and fearful I sound.

I wait, but the house remains silent. The only sound is a very faint scraping at the broken window, and I can see a shadow flashing at the edge, as if a stray branch from the overgrown garden is getting blown against the glass.

Pulling the blanket even tighter shut, I make my way out into the hallway and stop at the foot of the main staircase, looking up toward the landing. All I can see is a handrail, and some old paintings on the walls up there.

"Hello?" I say again, before realizing that I need to be a little louder. "Hello, is anyone there?"

The only reply is the continued scraping of the branch against the window.

There's still a part of me that wants to turn and run, but deep down I feel as if the person in this house only wanted to help me. Perhaps he's shy, or perhaps he's resting, or maybe he even stepped out for a while. I don't know why he would have operated on me himself, instead of calling an ambulance, but then I figure sometimes people don't want to draw attention to themselves, and that's definitely something I can appreciate. So I watch the top of the stairs for a moment longer, and then – almost without thinking – I start walking up.

"Hello?" I say yet again, keeping my eyes fixed on the railing at the top, in case I spot a hint of movement. "Is anyone here?"

The steps creak under my feet, and the branch continues to brush the window, but otherwise there's no sound at all. As I reach the halfway point and stop again, I'm starting to feel as if maybe the other person simply came and went in the night, saving my life and then rushing off into the darkness. That story's pretty improbable, but it's the only thing that even remotely makes sense right now. Or maybe *nothing* makes sense, and this whole situation is insane.

"My name's Maddie," I continue, speaking to the empty space at the top of the stairs, just in case anyone is listening. "Thank you for..."

My voice trails off, and I look down once again at my stitches. The wound still hurts, and there's still a lot of blood caked across the skin, but I can't deny that the torn skin has been forced back together. The stranger's work might not be neat, but it seems to have been effective.

He might even have saved my life.

"Thank you for helping me," I say finally, looking back up toward the top of the stairs. "I don't quite know what happened. I don't want to bother you, but... Thank you."

I wait.

Silence.

Maybe this guy is a real loner. Maybe he's some kind of weird reclusive super-surgeon who lives alone in an abandoned house, fixing up people who happen to come climbing through his window after getting stabbed.

Well, that explanation's no more crazy than

anything else I can come up with right now.

"I'm sorry I broke into your house," I continue. "Well, I didn't break in, not technically. The window was already broken, and I didn't think anybody lived here. There was such a bad storm last night, I was worried I was going to catch pneumonia out there. I know it was wrong to come in without asking, but I really didn't think anybody was here. Please, accept my apology about that. I didn't mean to disturb you at all."

I watch the doors, but there's still no sign of anyone. Maybe there's a figure hiding just out of view, listening to me, or maybe I'm talking to myself.

"Okay, then," I add, figuring that I should just take the cue. I turn to head back down. "I'll get going and -"

Suddenly I hear the bell ring again.

I freeze, and this time the sound continues for several more seconds, long enough for me to look back up and realize that it seems to be coming from an open doorway just to the left at the top of the stairs. I watch the doorway until the bell stops, and then I wait in case I hear any further sign of movement.

Footsteps, maybe, or even a voice.

All I hear, however, is silence.

I don't want to go any further up these stairs. If there's somebody up there, and if they helped me during the night, then it's clear they don't want to talk now. Even if this person fell asleep, I'm sure he'd have woken by now; after all, I've been calling out for several minutes. Maybe the bell is somehow his way of answering, although after a moment it occurs to me that he might be in trouble. There are so many possibilities, but I'm starting to think that I should at least check to make sure he's okay. After all, a psychopath would have just killed me already when I was unconscious.

What if he saved me, and then I leave just as he needs help in return?

Cautiously, then, I start making my way up to the landing. And just as I reach the top, and just as the floorboard creaks beneath my right foot, I hear the bell ring out again.

CHAPTER EIGHTEEN
DOCTOR CHARLES GRAZIER

Sunday September 30th, 1888

Catherine's bell rings, and I immediately open my eyes.

Silence.

No, the bell didn't ring.

In my fevered, barely rested state, I must have imagined the bell just as I was in danger of falling asleep. After dealing with Catherine's illness for so long, I have become accustomed to listening out for the bell at all hours. I have even been woken in the dead of night by the sound. I almost believe that if that bell rang, it could wake me from death itself.

The first rays of morning sun have begun to lighten the window, bringing the beginning of what promises to be a cool Sunday morning. No doubt the bells of the nearby church will ring out soon, calling the idiotic faithful to their service. How people can believe in such foolishness, I cannot imagine. Most people, I suppose, are simply idiots.

One should only believe in science. In rational things, things for which one has evidence.

I have been sitting here in my study for several hours now, ever since I left Catherine in her bed. My original plan had been to let her rest down in the basement, on the operating table, but I felt that she should be given a little more comfort, and that she should have the dignity of recovering in her own bedroom. This is why I carried her back up the stairs, taking care to not disturb her stitches, and it is why she now rests in her own bed, in her own room. When she eventually wakes, she will be in familiar surroundings, and she will feel as if she has emerged from a long nightmare.

The basement is a place of work, not fit for a lady.

I wanted to sit with her all night and all day, of course, but in truth I needed to come down here and get something to eat. There was some old bread in the kitchen, and the bread has been chased down with a glass of whiskey. The light at the window might tell me that morning has arrived, but in my heart I feel as if I am simply one more hour into a relentless night that has lasted several years. There will be a few more sunrises, I am sure, before I truly feel the darkness begin to lift.

Finally, exhausted in a way I have never felt before, I close my eyes again.

Catherine will be fine.

Suddenly I hear the bell ringing again, and my

eyes immediately flick open. I wait in silence, convinced that I must have misheard, that perhaps one part of my mind slipped into a dream before the rest. After all, the only bell in this house is the one that rests on the nightstand next to Catherine's bed, so that she might call for me. Since Catherine is deep in sedation, I know full well that she cannot possibly be calling me, yet even now the echo of the bell seems to fill my mind.

I look over at the open doorway, toward the hall, but the house is once again so very quiet.

There is only one possible explanation. I must be so utterly wracked by lack of sleep, I have begun to imagine things. My senses are not quite right, yet I cannot afford to sleep just now. I must remain awake for the next few days, so that I can be constantly available to tend to my darling Catherine. As I turn and look back toward the window, I remind myself that for now I am my wife's servant. There will be time to sleep later, when we are both recovered from this ordeal, but for now -

Suddenly the bell rings again.

I immediately rise from the armchair and turn to look toward the doorway.

It cannot be, and yet...

The house is silent once more, but this time I cannot so easily adjudge myself to have imagined the sound. Indeed, as I take a few more tentative steps toward the doorway, I fully expect to hear the bell again. And by the time I get to the threshold and look through to the main staircase, I feel more certain than ever that somebody did indeed ring the bell, which can only mean that my dear Catherine has somehow woken very early from her sedation. She must be in the most awful pain, yet I do not hear her crying out.

And then the bell rings yet again, this time for several seconds, almost as if Catherine knows of my doubts and wishes to affirm that she is indeed calling me.

"Catherine?" I whisper.

I am immediately shocked by the fear in my own voice.

"Catherine," I continue, raising my voice a little but still not quite believing what I can hear, "are you in need of attention?"

I wait, but now the house is silent.

Suddenly I realize that this is not the time to hesitate. I hurry to the stairs and up toward the landing, and by the time I'm halfway I hear the bell again. This time the sound lasts even longer than before, as if Catherine's desperation is becoming greater, so I start taking the stairs two at a time until I reach the landing and head along to her room. With each step, I become more and more convinced that she has somehow woken, that I perhaps misjudged the levels of sedation and she has woken in a fit of agony.

"My dear," I say as I reach the open doorway, "whatever has -"

The bell stops as soon as I see Catherine's body upon the bed.

She is absolutely still. Her neck has been slit, covered in thick red blood, and her face is turned this way. Her dead eyes stare almost, but not quite, into my own.

“Catherine,” I whisper, momentarily stilled by the shock of what I am seeing.

I step forward, although I stop again as I reach the bed.

Catherine's neck has indeed been cut from ear to ear, leaving a thin cut from which a great deal of blood has run. The top of her nightshirt has been stained red, as have the bedsheets and pillows. There is so much blood, in fact, that I already know without any doubt whatsoever that she must be dead. No body could survive such an outpouring, and a moment later I hear a faint dripping sound. Looking down, I see that spots of blood are dropping from the soaked sheets and landing on the bare floorboards.

For a moment I am frozen, too horrified to weep yet also too horrified to cry out. I simply cannot believe that this is real.

“Catherine!” I whisper, finally stepping closer and reaching out, desperately searching for some hint of life. I check her neck, but there is no pulse, and then I reach down to check her wrist. The leather manacles are still in place, since I unhooked them from the chair earlier and did not remember to remove them. I try to force two fingers beneath the manacles, to check for a pulse at Catherine's wrists, but I cannot reach.

And then I see the letter.

A folded piece of paper rests in Catherine's left hand, and my name is written on its front.

Again I freeze, too horrified to believe that any of this is really happening. After a few seconds, however, I reach out and take the piece of paper, and when I unfold it I find that it contains a note written in my dear wife's own hand. The script is faint and ragged in places, but it is most certainly hers:

> *My dearest darling Charles,*
>
> *There can be no pain greater than the pain of parting. Yet I know that we shall be reunited some day, long after these mortal bodies have lost their power to make us ache. We shall be together in whatever realm exists beyond the veil of death.*
>
> *I have experienced so much pain over the past few months, that it was no great difficulty to endure more during the procedure. I do not know how I woke, but I did, and then by some miracle I felt you set a scalpel next to my hand.*
>
> *I hid that scalpel, my dear, and I waited until you had returned me to this bed. And then I did what you see now, and by the time you read this letter the pain will be over. For me, at least. You must not blame yourself, and you must try to forgive me my act of deception.*
>
> *I suppose I have become desperate.*

I cannot stand what my illness has turned you into, and what you have become in your constant search for a cure. I cannot write the words, but I believe I understand what you have been doing, and my heart breaks.

Do not mourn, Charles, and do not follow me in haste. Bury me, my darling, and then live your life. I love you with all my heart, but I could not go on living like this. You have your health, and I implore you to cling to your life for so long as you are fit and healthy. You have my blessing to marry again, and I hope that you do. Perhaps a second wife would be able to give you children, and I know that the lack of a child is your one disappointment in our marriage.

Forgive me for what I have done. I know you did what you did out of love, but I could endure it no longer. The leather manacles prevent me cutting my wrists, so I shall have to work on my throat instead. Do not attempt to clean the sheets. They must be thrown away.

Goodbye, my darling.

Until next we meet.

Your ever-loving and devoted,

Catherine.

I read the note several times, struggling to make sense of its meaning. I know Catherine cannot have done something so awful, I know that there has to be another explanation, yet the evidence is before me. I left the manacles on Catherine's wrists when I brought her up, simply because I forgot to take them off, so evidently she opted to cut her throat instead. I cannot imagine what she must have been thinking, or how she could have done all of this while I was resting downstairs.

How did she even stay quiet while I was operating? It is inconceivable that she did not cry out, yet I can only suppose that she had endured so much pain for so long, she was able by the end to endure almost anything. Anything except hope.

"I had saved you," I whisper, as I feel tears welling in my eyes. "Catherine, I..."

My voice trails off, and a moment later the letter falls from my hands.

"I saved you," I continue, looking at her dead, glassy eyes. "I finally saved you. All you had to do was wait and let me guide you back to health. I saved you, I..."

Again, I cannot finish the sentence. Somehow the words catch in my throat, as I feel a strange tightening sensation in my chest. For a few seconds, I fear that I might collapse in a rush of sorrow, but then I begin to realize that in actual fact I feel intense anger.

"After all I did," I whisper, clenching my fists tight, "you lost faith. I told you the procedure would work this time. All you had to do was keep your faith in me a little longer, and everything would have been alright. I promise, I promise..."

As my anger builds, I have to hold back the urge to grab Catherine's lifeless body by the shoulders and shake her violently. I want to shout at her, to scream that she has left me too soon, yet at the same time I cannot possibly bring myself to hurt even one hair on her head.

"I was going to cure you!" I imagine myself screaming at her. "I was going to make you better!"

Finally, looking over at her bedside table, I spot the bell. Filled with a sudden burst of fury, I reach over and knock the bell away, sending it clattering to the ground.

I had done it.

I had finally saved her, and all was set to be good again in our lives.

I lunge at the bedside table again, this time grabbing it by its sides and then swinging it around, pushing it over so that Catherine's reading glasses and cups and trinkets are scattered across the carpet. And when even that does nothing to disperse my fury, I turn and grab the curtains, pulling them away with a furious cry and bringing the rod down as well, before finally I turn once more and – without thinking – smash my fists against the mirror on the dressing table, breaking the glass and cutting my hands.

Why couldn't she believe in me?

Why did she give up, just as I had finally found a way to cure her?

CHAPTER NINETEEN
MADDIE

Today

THIS IS THE ROOM WHERE THE RINGING SOUND CAME FROM, BUT IT'S EMPTY NOW.

Standing in the doorway, still hugging the blanket tight, I look through into a large, gloomy room. The walls are cracked and peeling, and the floorboards have been left uncovered to rot. There's a large bay window at the room's far end, with wooden boards covering the glass and only a crack of light managing to break through, but the curtains are on the floor and the rod looks to have been ripped down. There's a kind of old-fashioned dressing table against the far wall, although I can't help noticing that the glass has been smashed.

Stepping closer, I see faint dark stains on some of the glass shards. I feel more pieces of glass crunching beneath the soles of my shoes, and then I see that various cups and pieces of jewelry have been left on the carpet. Even the chandelier appears to have been partially ripped out from the ceiling, although it was left half-dangling as if somebody's fury finally faded.

It looks like someone went pretty nuts in here.

Making my way around the glass, I head over to take a look at the old metal bed. There are old, stained sheets still covering the mattress, and I can't help but notice a stale smell in the air.

I look down at all the junk on the floor, hoping that perhaps I'll spot a bell and that – at the same time – I'll find a breeze that might have caused the bell to ring. There's no bell on the carpet, however. I look at the bed's metal posts, but there's no bell there, nor is there one anywhere near the window. Opposite the bed there's an old fireplace, but I still don't see a bell. By the time I get to the center of the room and look around, however, I'm starting to feel a little uneasy, almost as if somebody is watching me.

There's no-one here, of course, and finally I find myself staring down at the empty bed.

I've never felt this sensation before, but I swear I can feel a pair of eyes looking straight back at me from the darkness. I can see the wall, so I know without a shadow of a doubt that there's nobody sitting on the bed, but at the same time I feel completely certain that there's a presence looking at me. This sensation is so certain, in fact, that I finally make my way around to the side of the bed and look closer, even resorting to waving my hand through the air to make absolutely sure that I'm not somehow missing a person.

I guess I'm just losing my mind.

After all, this is a pretty creepy house both inside and out, so it's not too hard to believe that the atmosphere has affected me. I reckon pretty much anyone would start getting jumpy in a place like this.

Still, I wave my hand above the bed a couple more times, just to make myself feel a little better, before finally taking a step back. I don't know what caused the bell sound, but then I guess I don't really *need* to know. In a big old house like this, with so many rooms and probably plenty of holes and cracks in the walls, there are lots of things that could cause a sound that seems like a bell. I've never been the kind of person who leaps to believe in the supernatural just because she can't find an explanation for something, so I'll just have to be content with not knowing.

Still, the sensation of dark, staring eyes is enough to give me the willies.

And then I spot the bell.

Resting on the edge of the bed's frame, there's a small golden bell.

Stepping closer, I look down at the bell and see to my surprise that – like everything else here – it's covered in dust. There's so much dust, in fact, that there's no way it could have been rung any time recently. Picking the bell up, I watch as some of the dust falls away. I hesitate, wondering whether it'd be right to break the silence of the house, but then I tell myself to stop being so superstitious.

So I ring the bell.

Just for a few seconds, just long enough for me to tell that it works. It sure sounds like the bell I heard earlier, but of course it can't be the same one. Figuring that there must be another bell somewhere, I set it down and step back, taking another look at the bed.

I still feel as if somebody is watching me, but I guess I'm just letting myself get a little spooked. Funny how easily that can happen.

I head back out to the landing, intending to go downstairs, but then I stop again as soon as I see that the opposite bedroom door is wide open. Maybe I wasn't paying attention earlier, but I swear that door was shut. I limp over and swing the door partially shut, mainly to reassure myself that I'd have heard a creaking sound if the door *had* moved. To my surprise, however, I find that this particular door – unlike all the others in the house so far – moves silently.

I look through and see that this room is fully furnished. There's a much nicer-looking wooden bed, along with wardrobes and chairs and even a desk next to the boarded-up window. Honestly, apart from the thick layer of dust that I quickly find coating the top of a chest of drawers, it's almost as if somebody has been living here recently. I step into the room and look around, before heading to the desk and seeing all sorts of beautiful old jewelry arrange on various stands.

There are earrings and necklaces, rings and even what looks like a tiara, and they're all glittering in the low light. I've never been around fancy jewelry before, but as I reach down and pick up one of the necklaces, I can't help thinking that these are real diamonds and real pearls. For a moment, as I hold the necklace up, I'm mesmerized by the beauty and opulence, and by the realization that in all my life I've probably never touched something so stunning.

And then, suddenly, I set the necklace down, shocked by the thought that I was considering...

No.

No, I wasn't considering taking anything.

I'm not a thief.

Trying to distract myself, I pick up a dusty old framed photo that's standing close to the jewelry. I have to wipe the grime away from the glass, but finally I see a very old, very faded image.

There are two people in the picture. One is an old man with a very intense stare, wearing old-fashioned clothes, while the other person is a frail, angry-looking woman sitting in front of him on a chair. She looks painfully thin, almost as if she was ill when the photo was taken. At the bottom of the image, somebody has scrawled the year 1888 in spidery, almost indecipherable handwriting.

There's another photo, this time showing a younger, happier-looking couple standing on what looks like some kind of clifftop. The difference in their faces – in their postures and their dress, in pretty much every aspect of them – is so great, it actually takes a few seconds before I realize that these are the same people from the first photo. Comparing them now, I can't even begin to imagine how two people could change from looking so happy to looking so utterly miserable, but I guess stuff like that happens sometimes.

These must have been the owners of the house. I can't imagine why their stuff would have been left here, but then maybe they had no children. Maybe they died a long time ago, and somehow the house ended up just standing here.

I set the photos down and turn to leave the room, but suddenly my foot catches against some kind of old case that has been left under the desk. I almost walk away without taking a closer look, but something about the battered old trunk – with one corner sticking out almost as if it was designed to trip somebody – makes me crouch down. My wound bites with a sharp pain, and I wince as I pull the case out a little further. There's plenty of dust on the top, and it takes a moment before I'm able to open the clasps and raise the lid.

There's nothing inside, of course.

I pull the case all the way out and check for another, but there's nothing. And then, just as I'm about to get to my feet, I see that there's what looks like a small handle set into one of the floorboards. The handle was hidden by the case at first, but now I reach down and give it a tug, only to find that a square hatch starts shuddering. I pull again, trying to jiggle the hatch open, but there's plenty of resistance and finally I stop as I realize that this thing probably requires proper tools if it's ever going to be pulled up.

Still, I've disturbed plenty of dust, and now I can see the square outline of the hatch's door. There's clearly some kind of hiding place here, in the floorboards under the desk, and I can't help wondering what might be down here. Probably nothing, but still...

I pull the handle a few more times, but the hatch seems to be stuck fast. I check for any kind of lock, although there doesn't seem to be anything in the way. I guess maybe the hatch door has simply warped over the years, and I'm pretty sure there's no way I'll be able to get it open. I still try a few more times, tugging several times until I finally realize that there seems to be something keeping the hatch firmly shut. Short of finding an ax and smashing the thing open, I'm pretty sure I'm done here.

Besides, I doubt there's anything interesting down there.

Getting to my feet, I turn and start heading back to the doorway. Somehow I feel even more exhausted than before, even though morning has come. I reach down and check my wound again, and to my relief I find that the stitches seem to be holding. For now, at least, although I'm worried they might come undone at any moment.

Then again, they seem pretty tight. Almost as if they were put in place by someone who knew what he was doing.

Seeing as I don't seem to have lost any more blood, I figure it's time to get out of this house. Whoever helped me with my injury, they're obviously not around, so I guess they don't want to be thanked in person.

I'll write a note, and then I'll leave and -

Suddenly I hear an almighty crashing sound over my shoulder, and I spin around just in time to see that the obstinately closed hatch has burst open of its own accord, sending splinters of broken wood scattering across the floor. And now, as I stare in shock, I see that the hatch is fully open, revealing a stash of old papers and books.

CHAPTER TWENTY
DOCTOR CHARLES GRAZIER

Sunday September 30th, 1888

"IT'S SO BEAUTIFUL OUT HERE," Catherine says, standing in the sunlight and watching the waves from the clifftop. After a moment, she turns to me and smiles. "Are you sure, Charles, that we can't move down here?"

"To Cornwall?"

Stepping over to her, I place a hand on her waist. I want to tell her that leaving London is impossible, that my work will bind me to the city, but for a few seconds I cannot help staring out at the beautiful sea and feeling a tug on my heart. This would be an idyllic place for us to live our lives.

"Never mind," Catherine says suddenly. "I am putting too much pressure on you. Forget I said anything."

"Perhaps we can manage it one day," I whisper,

even though I know that I am promising too much.

"Let's never grow old, Charles," she replies.

"Now you really *are* asking a lot," I point out.

"Fine," she says, sounding a little exasperated as she places her hands on my shoulders, "but if we must grow old, then let us at least not grow bitter, or angry. Let us always remain filled with the joy of life."

"I have no intention otherwise," I tell her with a smile.

"You must take this seriously!"

"I am."

"No, you're not." She stares up into my eyes, as if she is searching for something, and I fear I can see a note of concern in her expression. "People can become old and twisted, Charles," she continues finally. "I don't know how. Life, I suppose, batters one so very often, from all directions. I have seen it in members of my own family, I have witnessed the way they can be chipped away at until they despise the world. Let us never, ever become like that. Happy to the end?"

I open my mouth to make some humorous remark, but at the last moment I realize that this would perhaps be inappropriate. I must, instead, calm Catherine's fears.

"Happy to the end," I reply, and I see an instant wave of relief in her features.

"I think the photographer is ready now," she says, reaching down and taking my hand as we both turn to see the photographer waiting just a short distance away. "Now do try to smile like a normal person for once. You always look so terrified and unnatural when you're having your photograph taken."

"I do not!" I protest, although I know deep down that she has a point. "I'm simply not used to such things," I add, taking a moment to adjust my jacket so that I shall look more presentable. "How is one ever supposed to relax when one has one of those infernal cameras pointed in one's face."

Behind us, waves are crashing against the base of the cliff. Catherine was right when she said this place was idyllic, but the memory serves to remind me of the path not taken. After all, as I stir from these remembrances and find myself sitting alone in one of the spare bedrooms, I know full well that we never again visited Cornwall, not after that brief trip shortly after our marriage.

I blink, and the memory is gone.

It must be almost sunrise, and I have been sitting here for so long, delaying the moment when I must go back through and attend to Catherine's body. I have allowed myself to become lost in memories that seemed so real and so immediate, it was almost as if I was back there myself. Yet now, alone in the darkened room, I feel the full weight of the moment pushing down against my shoulders.

I only sat down to make some notes. I have one of my books open on my knees, and I take a moment to add some annotations concerning the most recent procedure. I have been keeping meticulous records of my work, complete with diagrams and notes concerning Catherine's recovery. I have also kept notes concerning my nocturnal activities, even going so far as to document the details of the whores I have killed. All these notes have greater value as a record of my endeavors, and I quite sure future generations will be able to look past the trivial details of the killings, and will instead focus on my achievements.

I make a few more notes, but in truth I am weary and I feel that I have explained myself enough. Setting the book aside, I take a moment to rest, before realizing that I am in danger of once more slipping into a comforting dream.

Getting to my feet, I'm about to go through to Catherine's bedroom, when I spot a familiar photograph resting on the dresser. I walk over and pick it up, and sure enough I find myself looking down at the picture that was taken during our trip to Cornwall all those years ago.

Catherine and I stare out of the photograph, looking so happy and carefree.

Where did those days go?

A moment later, I spot another photograph on the dresser, and this one sends a shudder through my chest. I was the one who suggested having our portrait re-done, around a year ago when Catherine's illness first began to show. At the time, we had not yet accepted that she was sick, but looking at the photographer now I can see the pain and fear etched into her features, and the fear in my own face. How did we go from being the happy, optimistic couple in the first photograph, to being the bitter souls in the second?

"People can become old and twisted, Charles," I hear Catherine's voice whispering in my mind. "Life, I suppose, batters one so very often, from all directions."

Turning, I look out through the doorway, across the landing toward the opposite bedroom. Even from here, I can see Catherine's dead body on her bed. I am sure I closed her eyes earlier before I left the room, but now her eyes are open and staring up at the ceiling.

She is the love of my life, and now I must attend to her ravaged and damaged corpse.

CHAPTER TWENTY-ONE
MADDIE

Today

GETTING DOWN ONTO MY KNEES, with my back to the door, I reach down into the open hatch and pick up one of the many notebooks.

The cover immediately starts to come away from the spine, and I take a little more care as I set the notebook down and open it to take a look at the pages. The book is filled with what look like medical diagrams, with pencil and ink sketches of body parts. There are a load of notes, too, handwritten at the sides, but the writing is really old-fashioned and to be honest I can barely make out any of the words.

"Kidney extraction," I whisper, trying to decipher one particular line, "along the... exterior... clavi... os..."

I'm not sure what the rest of the sentence says. It

might be medical jargon, or it might just be written in too spidery a hand, but after a moment I give up and try the next page. The writing here is no easier to understand, but at least I can make out the diagrams. And as I flick through some more pages, I see more and more sketches that seem to show procedures being carried out on a human body.

Pictures of kidneys.

Of open bodies.

Of a liver – I think – being removed from someone.

I don't know much about medical history, but I've got to admit to being quite surprised that such complicated procedures were being carried out back in the nineteenth century. Some of the images have dates scribbled next to them, suggesting that these notebooks were written in the year 1888. I don't think I've ever held anything so old, and finally I close the book and set if very carefully back in the space beneath the hatch.

Looking at the hinges of the hatch, I try to find a spring or some other mechanism that might explain how the whole thing suddenly sprang open with such force. There are small splinters of wood all around, so it's clear that the hatch opened violently, but I can't find anything that might explain what happened. It's as if, after my half-hearted attempts to get the hatch open myself, it finally decided that its time had come. Then again, I know such things are impossible, so I can only assume that some hidden system was at work.

I spend a few more minutes looking at another notebook, but again the writing is way too hard to read. I do manage to make out a name, however, written on the first page.

"Doctor Charles Grazier," I whisper.

At least, I think that's what it says.

"I don't know who you were, Charles Grazier," I continue, "but it looks like you were very busy."

And maybe influential, too. Glancing up at one of the framed pictures next to the jewelry, I realize that Grazier might be the man in the photos.

Suddenly I realize that these old notebooks have to be linked somehow to the other things I've experienced in this spooky old house. Reaching down, I brush my fingers against the thick loops of black wire that were used to stitch my wound, and I'm starting to think that whoever lives in this house now must be some kind of surgeon. After a moment I turn and look back toward the open doorway, but there's still no sign of anyone. Glancing around, however, I start wondering whether there might be somebody watching from somewhere, or even hidden cameras.

Sure, the idea's crazy, but so's everything else that's happened here tonight.

Quickly putting the notebooks back how I found them, I close the hatch and get to my feet. I keep telling myself that I'm probably overreacting – I *hope* I'm overreacting – but I start backing away as I feel a tingling sensation running over my shoulders and up to the back of my neck. Whatever's going on in this house, I really don't think I want to stick around and find out.

"So I'm gonna go now," I say out loud, and I can hear the fear in my own voice now. "I won't tell anyone about this, okay? Thank you for helping me, but I promise I won't breathe a word to anyone. I don't know what's going on here, but I don't need to know. Deal?"

I wait, but the house remains silent.

I really think my mysterious savior is away right now, in which case it'd probably be wise to get out of here before he comes back.

Turning, I head toward the door.

Before I've managed even two steps, however, I hear a faint creaking sound over my shoulder, along with what sounds like jewelry rattling slightly. I freeze, and now the sounds have stopped, but after a moment I can't help turning back to take a look.

I close the hatch.

I swear I close it, but now it's open again.

And on the dresser nearby, some of the beautiful necklaces are swinging just slightly, as if they were touched a moment ago.

I wait, looking around, but there's definitely nobody else here.

I guess there must have just been a strong breeze. One that was strong enough to make the necklaces sway. And to open a heavy wooden hatch.

"Okay," I mumble, "thanks for everything."

With that, I turn and hurry out of the room, trying not to panic but still picking up speed as I head to the top of the stairs. To be honest, I'm pretty worried that I'll suddenly hear another noise, or that a hand will suddenly grab my shoulder from behind, and as I head down the stairs I can't help thinking that somebody must be watching me from somewhere. Even if the guy who lives here isn't around right now, he might have little cameras hidden in the cracks in the walls. I mean, maybe he's totally friendly and benign, and he only wanted to help me and I'm being a totally suspicious bitch, but right now I'm filled with an overwhelming sense that I need to get the hell out of this house. It's not my mystery to solve.

When I get back downstairs, I hurry to the front room and grab my clothes. They're still pretty wet, but this time I don't even hesitate to start putting them back on. I wince a little as I feel the cold fabric against my skin, but at the same time I keep glancing over my shoulder, just in case a figure appears in the doorway. In fact, no matter how much I tell myself to keep from panicking, I'm starting to get increasingly convinced that I'm not alone in this house. I finish getting dressed, and then I grab my bag and haul it over my shoulder before hurrying back out to the hallway.

I glance up the stairs as I head to the window, but there's still no sign of anyone.

Climbing back out through the broken window, I struggle a little as I feel a few twinges of pain in my waist. Still, it's light outside now, and morning sunshine has chased away the rain.

I push my bag out first, before clambering through the window and dropping down into some bushes in the garden.

I land awkwardly, feeling a brief pain in my ankle, and I somehow lose my footing and slam down butt-first against the ground.

Letting out a gasp of pain, I immediately start

getting to my feet, but as I do so something slips out of my shirt pocket and falls down against the damp grass.

Earrings.

I freeze as I see a set of beautiful, glittering earrings.

They're clearly from inside the house, but I have no idea how they ended up in my shirt pocket. I swear I didn't take them, but they look like they match the jewelry from the room upstairs.

Reaching down, I pick them up and take a closer look, and I'm no jewelry expert but these things sure look like they're worth some serious money.

I just don't understand how they ended up in my shirt pocket, when my shirt was downstairs in that empty room all night.

And now here I am, poor and penniless and homeless, on my knees with what seem to be some valuable earrings in my hands.

For a few seconds, I can't help but imagine the possibilities. It's almost as if these earrings were deliberately given to me, as if fate has been leading me to this point so that I could be offered a second chance. I actually start imagining some secretive figure creeping through the house, stitching my wound and then – for some reason – slipping some jewelry into my clothes. That doesn't make much sense, but then nothing about this crazy night makes sense right now.

I turn and look back up at the broken window, and then I look down at the earrings again.

I can't take them.

I just can't.

However and whyever they ended up in my pocket, I'm no thief and I can't just waltz off with these things. They're not mine and there must have been some kind of mistake. At the same time, I keep imagining a hidden hand slipping the earrings into my pocket, as if they were somehow intended as a gift. I know that I should toss them back through the broken window, but there's definitely a part of me that's already starting to wonder just how valuable they might be, and what I could do with the money.

"It's a tough world," I hear Alex saying in the back of my mind. "You've got to take your chances wherever and whenever you get them. There's no time for morals, not if you want to survive."

"But I'm not a thief," I imagine myself replying.

"Get over yourself, Maddie."

That's what she'd say.

"Get over yourself and grow up. Do you know what happens to people with morals out here on the street? They die, Maddie. They starve, or they get knifed, or they just fade away to nothing. You need to look after yourself, 'cause let me promise you, no-one else is gonna look after you."

She'd want me to take the earrings. She'd probably have taken the rest of the jewelry, too. She'd be coming up with plan after plan after plan, and she wouldn't even bother to think about whether what she was doing was right or wrong. She'd just take the jewelry and cash it all in, and she wouldn't even look back.

I can't do that, though.

These earrings aren't mine. If I take them, I don't think I'll ever be able to live with myself.

CHAPTER TWENTY-TWO
DOCTOR CHARLES GRAZIER

Sunday September 30th, 1888

ONCE I HAVE WRAPPED CATHERINE'S BODY IN A SILK SHEET, there is nothing left for me to do other than to set a patch of fabric across her face. Still, I hesitate for a moment, staring down at her features until finally I realize that I am simply delaying the inevitable.

I place a corner of the sheet over her face, and then I take a step back.

It is done.

I cleaned away as much of the blood as I could manage. I spent several hours washing her body, and then I dressed her in one of her favorite shawls. I think I expected that the process would bring me a little peace, but in truth the opposite is true: I have felt continued rage and shock and anger, to the extent that I now wonder whether this shall be my perpetual state for the rest of my life. I want to grab Catherine by the shoulders and shake her until her life is restored, and then I want to make her see that I was right.

I want to hear her voice again.

I want her to tell me she's sorry, and that she believes in my work.

Soon I shall have to contact another doctor and have Catherine declared dead. There will be questions, of course, concerning the state of her body, and in particular concerning the unorthodox treatments to which she has been subjected. I imagine I shall be able to avoid any probing questions, thanks to my status and my connections in the medical field. In the unlikely event that the police become involved, perhaps the whole thing shall unravel, and perhaps I shall even be accused of murdering those whores.

Now that Catherine is gone, I scarcely care one way or the other.

Still, perhaps I can wait until morning before bringing the outside world into our home. I should like one final, calm night here, so that I might remember how things once were. Catherine would like that, too. I feel as if I have been fighting for so long, against such an implacable enemy, against the very cancer that consumed her body and grew through her bones...

I must rest now.

I am so tired, I do not think that even death will be quiet enough.

Turning, I head toward the door, although I stop when I see the bell on the floor. My anger has subsided a little now, or at least paused for a while, so I reach down and pick the bell up. It rings one more time as I set it on the nightstand, and then it falls silent. I suppose it shall never ring again, not now that Catherine is gone, and I might very well decide to have it placed in her coffin. Not out of some morbid belief that it might be needed again, but rather because I simply cannot think of anywhere else that might be suitable for it to rest. Over the past few months, after all, that bell has been constantly at Catherine's side. There were times when the cancer rendered her unable to speak, so she could communicate through the bell alone. It was almost a part of her.

I turn again, but this time a stray thought stops me in my tracks.

I pause for a moment, before turning and looking back over at Catherine's body. Although I desperately want to leave her in peace, I cannot help but wonder whether the kidney is taking to its new home. Indeed, although I know that Catherine's death means such processes will be interrupted, there is a part of me that remains curious.

Finally I head back over and move the sheet aside, before shifting the shawl back until I can see the stitches in my dead wife's abdomen. Everything looks satisfactory so far, and if she were alive I would be very confident that I had achieved my goals. Still, I cannot help but reach down and start unpicking the stitches with my bare hands, unthreading them carefully from her body until the wound begins to open. Once I have undone all the stitching, I pull the flaps of skin aside, and I feel a shudder pass through my chest as soon as I see the alien kidney that I put in place earlier.

The kidney looks darker than the rest of Catherine's organs.

More dead.

That is not possible, of course.

I reach down and start turning the kidney around, determined to prove to myself that the operation would have been a success. What I find, however, is that not only has the stitching begun to come loose, but that one side of the kidney appears to be deteriorating much faster than the other. Even as I turn the organ around in my hands, patches of meat are crumbling away into my hands. And when I tilt the kidney so that I might see the other side, I am horrified to watch as an entire section sloughs away from the bottom and falls into Catherine's abdominal cavity.

This kidney is dead, and I fear it would have died regardless of Catherine's health.

No.

No, I must not doubt myself.

I performed the transplant perfectly, and it is clear that the kidney is simply reacting swiftly to the death of its host. Putting aside my doubts, I force myself to remember that there is much about the human body that I do not understand, and I quickly realize that the kidney is most likely more sensitive to the changes that have begun to occur. If Catherine still lived, and if her heart could still pump blood around her body, the kidney would be thriving.

Yes, of course.

That is the explanation.

If only she had lived to see that I was right. Her survival would have been my greatest triumph, and men such as Thomas Culpepper would have dropped to their knees when they heard what I had done.

Now, however, there is nothing to show them. And I most certainly do not intend to share my new-found knowledge. Perhaps other lives could be saved, but why should I care?

"Why couldn't you have waited?" I whisper, taking a step back as I see that there is once again blood caked all over my hands. After a moment, I look at my wife's dead face. "My darling Catherine, what haste compelled you to rid yourself of this world? I was right, you would have seen that, you just needed to give me more time!"

Kneeling next to the bed, I kiss the side of her face. Her skin is cold already, but I cannot help kissing her again and again, all the way up past her ear and onto her forehead. Tears run from my eyes and drip onto her dead features, but I only wipe away the first couple before realizing that there are in fact too many. I kiss her forehead several more times, while wrapping my arms around her corpse and hugging her tight.

"I was going to save you!" I sob, unable to contain my sorrow for even a moment longer. "We'd have been happy again! You only had to wait while I saved you!"

Yet even as I speak these words, I know they are hollow. For Catherine is gone, and even I – the greatest surgeon in all of London – can have no hope of ever bringing her back. I must simply arrange certain matters in my life, and then join her in whatever place comes next. As I continue to hug and kiss her dead body, I know without a shadow of doubt that I cannot live without her.

One thing is certain, then. This life of mine is done.

CHAPTER TWENTY-THREE
MADDIE

Today

MY HEART IS POUNDING as I walk out of the shop, and I feel as if I might be about to faint. But somehow, despite my trembling knees and the pain in my waist, I make it to the corner and slip down the alley, and then I finally take a moment to re-count the cash in my trembling hands.

Two hundred and seventy-five pounds.

I count it again, then again, and then suddenly I stuff it all into my pocket and look around to make sure nobody noticed. My mind is racing so hard and so fast, I can barely think straight.

I don't think I've ever held so much money in my hands before. When the guy in the shop told me how much he'd pay me for the earrings, I struggled to keep a straight face. He asked a lot of questions, of course, and

I'm not convinced that the deal was quite on the up-and-up. There are probably loads of regulations about buying and selling antiques – and he said these are definitely antique earrings – and I kept expecting him to demand proof of where the jewelry had come from. The fact that he didn't ask for any proof at all makes me think, in fact, that he must be pretty dodgy himself. He obviously thought they were stolen, but apparently at the end of the day he didn't care too much.

Whatever.

He seemed happy, and I got what I needed.

I was expecting maybe a hundred pounds at most. The worst part is, the guy probably saw me coming from a mile off, and I'm pretty sure the earrings must have been worth even more than he gave me. Still, there's no way I'm going to complain. Even now, I can't help putting my hand into my pocket to double-check not only that the money is still there, but that it's real at all. There's definitely a part of me that think I might suddenly wake up, cold and alone on the floor in that house – and find that the past few hours have all been a dream.

Alex would be proud of me.

No, Alex *will* be proud of me, when I find her and show her what I've got.

Although if I tell her about all the other jewelry in the house, which must be worth thousands at the same rate, she'd probably be furious at me for not cleaning the place out.

Still, I'm no thief.

One day, I'll buy another set of earrings and take

them back to that house on Cromwell Street. I might even buy two, just to set things right. I'm not a thief, I swear I'm not, but right now this money might be enough for me to get back on my feet. I can buy a bus ticket and go to find Alex, and I'm sure she'll know how we can use what's left to really lift ourselves up off the streets. I guess maybe I'm being a little optimistic, but I don't suppose that really matters right now. What matters is that I actually have some money.

And I'll pay it back, I swear.

I'm not a thief.

The earrings were literally slipped into my pocket, which means somebody wanted me to have them. I have no idea why that might be, but I guess it's not my job to solve the mystery. Whatever's going on in that house, I'm grateful for the help I received but I really just want to keep away. Maybe there's some reclusive surgeon living there in squalor, casually doling out free jewelry to anyone who happens to climb through his window. I'm sure that's not the truth, but it's clear that *something* weird is happening there.

I need to stop overthinking this.

Obviously the owner of the house wanted me to have the earrings, and I should just be grateful.

Once I've checked yet again that the money is safely in my pocket, I head out of the alley and start making my way along the street. I don't even know where I'm going right now, but I *do* know that I have to make sure I don't splurge the money. The best option might be to go to a bus stop or a train station and try to figure out how I'm going to get to Stratford. Alex has always said that if she can get just a couple of hundred pounds together, she can buy things to sell at a market, and then she'll be able to get her life back on-track. If we work together, we might even -

Suddenly I stop in my tracks as I see yellow police tape fluttering in the breeze at the end of the street. A moment later I spot a couple of officers next to a police car, and one of them turns to look this way.

I immediately turn and start walking back the other way. Instantly, I realize that I'm acting suspiciously, but I figure I just need to get away. The police are obviously investigating something that happened in the neighborhood, so I doubt they'd give a damn about me, but there's always a danger that they might decide to make my life difficult. And if they began to scrutinize me at all – especially with all this cash in my pocket – they could make my life very *very* difficult. As I reach the end of the street I look over my shoulder, and I feel a flash of relief as I see that the police don't seem to be coming after me.

I watch the fluttering tape for a moment, before taking a left and heading along a different street. After just a couple of paces, however, I stop as I see that there's a TV crew ahead, with a news reporter talking into the camera. Whatever's happened around here, it seems to be big news. I watch for a few seconds, before hearing shuffling steps nearby and turning to find that an old man has come out of a house and is leaning against a bin as he too watches the news crew.

"What happened?" I stammer.

He turns to me.

"Do you know?" I continue, trying to force a smile. "Did something bad happen?"

"A girl got killed," he explains. "Someone found her this morning at sunrise, a couple of streets away. Didn't you hear about it on the news?"

Shocked, I shake my head.

"Was it an accident?" I ask.

"An accident?" He rolls his eyes. "I doubt it. Not after what they've been saying on the news."

"What have they been saying?"

"She was murdered. All cut up, like, with a knife."

I feel a shudder pass through my chest as I think back to my encounter with that guy last night. The guy who put a knife in my waist and almost killed me.

"How exactly was she killed?" I ask, trying to hide the fact that I'm panicked.

"They're saying it was pretty nasty," the man replies. "They're not giving out all the details, not yet. I heard she was all sliced in the belly, though. They say it was real horrible, and that -"

"Harold!" a woman's voice calls out from inside. "Are you coming or what?"

"Hang on!" he yells, before stepping over to me. "It's all over the news this morning," he continues, lowering his voice a little. "Haven't you been watching? It's the top story after the details came out. They haven't identified her yet, but that's probably just 'cause they've gotta inform the family first. If she had a family, this is. A lot of these street kids haven't got anyone at all. Maybe they'll just release the details later on."

"What details?" I ask.

"How the poor girl died. They say she was only a kid. Fifteen, sixteen, something like that. It shouldn't be happening, not in the modern world. Kids shouldn't be out there with nowhere to go and no-one to look after them, forced to sell themselves to whatever shady characters dangle some cash in front of their noses. It's not right."

"She was a prostitute?"

"They're not saying that, but everyone knows," he replies. "You see them all the time, up and down this street. It's as clear as the nose on your face. They're flaunting it, selling it, you name it."

"So a customer killed her?"

"She wasn't just killed," he continues, before miming a slicing motion across his belly. "From what I've heard, she was all cut up and she'd had all this horrible stuff done to her. Bits taken out, if you know what I mean. God bless her soul, but it's not right. A mate of mine said he saw some blood on the ground all the way up in Burgess Road. Sounds like the killer was a real butcher. From what I heard..."

He looks around again, as if he's still worried about being overheard, and then he leans even closer.

"From what I heard," he adds, "she got her guts ripped out right there on the street. Like an animal. All spread out everywhere. She was killed right there in the open, under a street-light, and no-one saw a thing. And you know what the world's like. If they don't catch the bugger soon, he'll kill again."

"Why would someone do such an awful thing?"

I ask with a shudder.

"It's a copycat."

"I'm sorry?"

He leans closer. "My mate at the paper says it's an exact copy of a murder that happened here over a hundred years ago."

"That's crazy," I point out.

"You know what's even crazier?" He turns and looks toward the flashing police lights, and I follow his gaze. "It's just like those murders that happened here back then," he continues. "Of course, the bloody papers are having a field day. The jackals love something like this, don't they? They've got no respect for the dead. I bet you a bunch of those dirty buggers are already trying to hack into her phone and her internet. That's what they're like, isn't it?"

"Harold!" the woman yells from inside. "Come and see this! It's on the telly! There's a helicopter! Our house was just on!"

He mutters something about having to go and watch, and about how it's important for me to stay safe, and then he heads into the house, leaving me shellshocked on the pavement. I watch the flashing lights for a moment, before starting to make my way along the street. No matter how many times I try to tell myself that this was all a coincidence, I can't help wondering whether I might have had a close encounter with the killer last night.

If I hadn't managed to kick him away, maybe I'd be the one who ended up getting killed and mutilated by some maniac.

As I walk along the street I pass camera crews and loiterers, gawpers and concerned locals leaning against their garden gates. People are even watching from the upstairs windows of nearby houses, as if everyone in this part of London wants to see what's happening. Up ahead there are more police vans arriving, along with a couple of trucks that have probably brought forensics teams to the area. This is turning into a major operation, and I'm actually a little stunned by the scene. It takes almost a full minute, in fact, before I realize that I'm wandering too close.

I take a detour across the road, toward a row of shops. Even here, however, there are people standing around and watching the scene, and whispering theories to one another. Trying to ignore them, I slip through the crowd, until suddenly I stop as I see some TV screens in a nearby shop window. Each TV is tuned to a news channel, and each channel is covering the story of the murder. They have their own approaches, of course, but one in particular grabs my attention with its lurid banner:

WOMAN, 23, STABBED TO DEATH IN WHITECHAPEL.

And another:

WHITECHAPEL MURDER LINKED TO BLACK MARKET ORGAN TRADE?

My thoughts immediately start racing as I think back to the man who attacked me last night. He only got the tip of his knife a couple of inches into my body, but I'm sure he'd have done more if he'd had the chance. I barely managed to fight him off and run, but now I can't help wondering whether I met the same shadowy figure who apparently killed a woman later in the evening.

And then I spot another banner on one of the other news channels.

Stepping closer to the window, I stare in horror at the 'Breaking News' at the bottom of one of the screens:

JACK THE RIPPER'S BACK IN LONDON!

CHAPTER TWENTY-FOUR
DOCTOR CHARLES GRAZIER

Sunday September 30th, 1888

NOW MORNING HAS ARRIVED, I can hear the cacophony of London outside the house. This will be the final morning of my life, so whereas I would usually be annoyed by such loudness, this time I stand in the hallway and listen to all the shouts and yells. London is loud and busy, and I dare say it shall continue to be loud and busy for as long as the city itself exists. Long beyond my day, for certain.

Everything is ready.

Catherine's body has been wrapped and left on the bed, along with a note detailing every aspect of her medical condition. I have asked in the note for there to be no autopsy, to spare Catherine the indignity of being cut open by men she did not know, but I doubt this request will be respected. Someone like Thomas

Culpepper – indeed, perhaps Culpepper himself – will carve into her and look at all the aspects of my work. This cannot be avoided, but I curse their names regardless. And I am quite sure that they will not understand the groundbreaking treatment that I developed.

One day, the name Charles Grazier will be famous the world over, once my journals have been properly read by the great men of future days. If I could not be so grandly lauded in life, then I take some comfort from the knowledge that such will be so after my death. There shall be books about my great work, and whole institutes named after me. Perhaps the people of my own time are timid and ill-equiped to recognize true brilliance in those who tower above them, but I trust that men of the future shall have their eyes a little more open. I had not intended to leave evidence of my accomplishments, yet that is precisely what I have ended up doing, in carefully annotated notebooks that shall be discovered after my death. In these notebooks, men shall learn of my great achievements in treating Catherine. I shall be mentioned in the same breaths as Newton and Gallileo and Da Vinci.

And here I am now, hesitating too long.

In truth, there is nothing left for me to do other than to go into the kitchen and perform one final, ghastly little ritual.

Turning, I step through the doorway and over to the kitchen table, where I have arranged a simple bowl with a scalpel at its side. As I sit down, I run through the plan one final time. I shall cut my wrists over the bowl, and then I shall go upstairs and settle myself next to Catherine on our marital bed. By the time our bodies are found, I shall have joined Catherine in the next life, and the horrors of this world will be forgotten. And now, as I take up the scalpel and tilt my left wrist to better see where I must cut, I feel a tremendous sense of calm starting to settle upon my shoulders. Soon, Catherine and I shall be together and -

Suddenly I hear the sound of breaking glass, followed by a loud and heavy thud.

I immediately turn and look toward the doorway, and for several seconds I sit in shocked silence and listen to a series of stumbling footsteps. There's a grunting sound too, a kind of breathless gasping, and finally the steps start heading down into the basement. It is almost as if a pig has entered the house.

A moment later I look down at the floorboards, and I realize I can hear somebody down there in the room beneath the kitchen.

Getting to my feet, I feel a rush of panic in my chest. I head over to the doorway and look out into the hall, and to my horror I see that the half-circle window has indeed been shattered. Stepping forward, I reach down and pick up one of the many shards of glass that have fallen upon the floor. I tell myself that this must be an illusion, that I am imagining the intrusion, but suddenly the glass shard catches against my finger and tears the skin, and I watch as a bead of blood starts dribbling down to the palm of my hand.

Downstairs, in the basement, somebody is moving about.

I should run to the front door and out into the street, so that I might call for the attention of a police officer. However, an officer of the law might have certain questions about what is going on inside the house, and might prevent me from achieving my end alongside Catherine upstairs.

Determined to keep order for at least a little longer, then, I head to the desk next to the stairs and I take a letter-opener from one of the drawers. This should be enough for me to defend myself, should the need arise, although I assume the intruder is likely a cowardly child. I have heard of criminal thugs sending children into houses to steal whatever they might find, but I have absolutely no sympathy for thieves. I shall certainly not hesitate to gut this child if necessary. I might be in my sixth decade now, but that does not mean I am a pushover.

How dare some homeless wretch break into my home?

"You there!" I shout as I reach the top of the wooden steps, looking down into the basement. "This is private property! You have one chance to come out, else I shall not be answerable for my actions!"

I wait, but now I hear nothing at all. Perhaps the little thief is hiding. Perhaps he even realizes that he has chosen the wrong house to attack. I imagine he is shivering with fear, terrified that he has finally met his match. I am quite sure that these little thieves always crumble when they are confronted by somebody of real force and character.

"You have been warned!" I continue, as I start

making my way down the steps. "I am not a man to be meddled with! Do you hear me? You picked the wrong house this morning!"

By the time I get to the basement, I am filled with a rare fury. This is supposed to be a peaceful morning, yet an intruder has chosen to break into the sanctuary of my home. As I step out across the basement and make my way toward the stone operating table at the center, I adjust my grip on the knife. I look around, so that this little monster cannot get a jump on me, but I suppose he must be hiding behind one of the pillars. Stepping carefully around the side of the table, therefore, I prepare myself to apprehend the intruder.

"You'd be better off running!" I call out, while glancing toward the benches and seeing that none of my scalpels are missing. "I'm not afraid to use force, young lad! You'll get what's coming to you if -"

Suddenly I hear a scraping sound from the far end of the room. I turn and look toward the farthest, shadowed part of the basement, which is where I keep my ice cases and assorted other items. To my surprise, I realize I can hear a continued slurping sound coming from the darkness, and I think I can just about make out the shape of a figure crouched on the ground, bent over and trembling violently. Immediately, I realize with a shudder that this figure appears rather larger than a child.

"Who are you?" I shout, determined to strike an imposing figure as I march across the basement. "I'll have you know I was a boxer in my youth. It's a brave man who brings a fight to Doctor Charles Grazier! A brave man or a fool, anyway."

I stop once I'm past the stone slab, and in truth I am starting to feel rather alarmed by the sight of this shabby figure. Now that I can see him more clearly, I realize that he is hunched over an upturned ice case, and I believe he might have emptied out the particular case in which I have been storing the unused body parts cut from the bodies of the dead whores. I can hear a chewing sound, too, and finally I take a couple more steps forward as I try to see exactly what is happening.

Suddenly, as if he has only now heard my approach, the hunched figure gets to his feet and turns to me.

To my horror, I see that he is a wretched fellow wearing a black suit that has clearly seen better days. His most striking aspect is a set of dark, soulless eyes, and I watch as he straightens up and steps toward me. As he emerges from the shadows, I realize that he is indeed holding one of the older unused uteruses in his hands, one that I took out of a Spitalfields whore a few weeks back. A moment later he raises the old uterus to his bloodied mouth and bites down, causing putrid black liquid to burst from the flesh and dribble down his wrists.

"Who are you?" I stammer, holding the knife up as I take a step back. "What are you doing in my house?"

"Who am I?" he asks, before grinning and – in the process – revealing a blood-stained mouth with flecks of torn human tissue stuck between his teeth. "Haven't you guessed yet?" he gasps, still smiling even though he seems to be in pain. "I'm the man they're calling Jack the Ripper!"

Coming Soon

IN DARKNESS DWELL

(THE HOUSE OF JACK THE RIPPER BOOK 2)

Lost and alone on the streets of London, and in desperate danger, Maddie finally realizes that she might have to do the one thing that goes against everything she believes in.

Meanwhile, more than a century earlier, Doctor Charles Grazier is forced to deal with a man whose capacity for violence and cruelty seems to know no limit, just as London begins to be gripped by the horror of Jack the Ripper.

Also by Amy Cross

The Soul Auction

"I saw a woman on the beach. I watched her face a demon."

Thirty years after her mother's death, Alice Ashcroft is drawn back to the coastal English town of Curridge. Somebody in Curridge has been reviewing Alice's novels online, and in those reviews there have been tantalizing hints at a hidden truth. A truth that seems to be linked to her dead mother.

"Thirty years ago, there was a soul auction."

Once she reaches Curridge, Alice finds strange things happening all around her. Something attacks her car. A figure watches her on the beach at night. And when she tries to find the person who has been reviewing her books, she makes a horrific discovery.

What really happened to Alice's mother thirty years ago? Who was she talking to, just moments before dropping dead on the beach? What caused a huge rockfall that nearly tore a nearby cliff-face in half? And what sinister presence is lurking in the grounds of the local church?

Also by Amy Cross

American Coven

He kidnapped three women and held them in his basement. He thought they couldn't fight back. He was wrong...

Snatched from the street near her home, Holly Carter is taken to a rural house and thrown down into a stone basement. She meets two other women who have also been kidnapped, and soon Holly learns about the horrific rituals that take place in the house. Eventually, she's called upstairs to take her place in the ice bath.

As her nightmare continues, however, Holly learns about a mysterious power that exists in the basement, and which the three women might be able to harness. When they finally manage to get through the metal door, however, the women have no idea that their fight for freedom is going to stretch out for more than a decade, or that it will culminate in a final, devastating demonstration of their new-found powers.

Also by Amy Cross

The Ash House

Why would anyone ever return to a haunted house?

For Diane Mercer the answer is simple. She's dying of cancer, and she wants to know once and for all whether ghosts are real.

Heading home with her young son, Diane is determined to find out whether the stories are real. After all, everyone else claimed to see and hear strange things in the house over the years. Everyone except Diane had some kind of experience in the house, or in the little ash house in the yard.

As Diane explores the house where she grew up, however, her son is exploring the yard and the forest. And while his mother might be struggling to come to terms with her own impending death, Daniel Mercer is puzzled by fleeting appearances of a strange little girl who seems drawn to the ash house, and by strange, rasping coughs that he keeps hearing at night.

The Ash House is a horror novel about a woman who desperately wants to know what will happen to her when she dies, and about a boy who uncovers the shocking truth about a young girl's murder.

Also by Amy Cross

Haunted

Twenty years ago, the ghost of a dead little girl drove Sheriff Michael Blaine to his death.

Now, that same ghost is coming for his daughter.

Returning to the small town where she grew up, Alex Roberts is determined to live a normal, quiet life. For the residents of Railham, however, she's an unwelcome reminder of the town's darkest hour.

Twenty years ago, nine-year-old Mo Garvey was found brutally murdered in a nearby forest. Everyone thinks that Alex's father was responsible, but if the killer was brought to justice, why is the ghost of Mo Garvey still after revenge?

And how far will the real killer go to protect his secret, when Alex starts getting closer to the truth?

Haunted is a horror novel about a woman who has to face her past, about a town that would rather forget, and about a little girl who refuses to let death stand in her way.

Also by Amy Cross

The Curse of Wetherley House

"If you walk through that door, Evil Mary will get you."

When she agrees to visit a supposedly haunted house with an old friend, Rosie assumes she'll encounter nothing more scary than a few creaks and bumps in the night. Even the legend of Evil Mary doesn't put her off. After all, she knows ghosts aren't real. But when Mary makes her first appearance, Rosie realizes she might already be trapped.

For more than a century, Wetherley House has been cursed. A horrific encounter on a remote road in the late 1800's has already caused a chain of misery and pain for all those who live at the house. Wetherley House was abandoned long ago, after a terrible discovery in the basement, something has remained undetected within its room. And even the local children know that Evil Mary waits in the house for anyone foolish enough to walk through the front door.

Before long, Rosie realizes that her entire life has been defined by the spirit of a woman who died in agony. Can she become the first person to escape Evil Mary, or will she fall victim to the same fate as the house's other occupants?

Also by Amy Cross

The Ghosts of Hexley Airport

Ten years ago, more than two hundred people died in a horrific plane crash at Hexley Airport.

Today, some say their ghosts still haunt the terminal building.

When she starts her new job at the airport, working a night shift as part of the security team, Casey assumes the stories about the place can't be true. Even when she has a strange encounter in a deserted part of the departure hall, she's certain that ghosts aren't real.

Soon, however, she's forced to face the truth. Not only is there something haunting the airport's buildings and tarmac, but a sinister force is working behind the scenes to replicate the circumstances of the original accident. And as a snowstorm moves in, Hexley Airport looks set to witness yet another disaster.

Also by Amy Cross

The Girl Who Never Came Back

Twenty years ago, Charlotte Abernathy vanished while playing near her family's house. Despite a frantic search, no trace of her was found until a year later, when the little girl turned up on the doorstep with no memory of where she'd been.

Today, Charlotte has put her mysterious ordeal behind her, even though she's never learned where she was during that missing year. However, when her eight-year-old niece vanishes in similar circumstances, a fully-grown Charlotte is forced to make a fresh attempt to uncover the truth.

Originally published in 2013, the fully revised and updated version of *The Girl Who Never Came Back* tells the harrowing story of a woman who thought she could forget her past, and of a little girl caught in the tangled web of a dark family secret.

Also by Amy Cross

The Devil, the Witch and the Whore
(The Deal book 1)

"Leave the forest alone. Whatever's out there, just let it be. Don't make it angry."

When a horrific discovery is made at the edge of town, Sheriff James Kopperud realizes the answers he seeks might be waiting beyond in the vast forest. But everybody in the town of Deal knows that there's something out there in the forest, something that should never be disturbed. A deal was made long ago, a deal that was supposed to keep the town safe. And if he insists on investigating the murder of a local girl, James is going to have to break that deal and head out into the wilderness.

Meanwhile, James has no idea that his estranged daughter Ramsey has returned to town. Ramsey is running from something, and she thinks she can find safety in the vast tunnel system that runs beneath the forest. Before long, however, Ramsey finds herself coming face to face with creatures that hide in the shadows. One of these creatures is known as the devil, and another is known as the witch. They're both waiting for the whore to arrive, but for very different reasons. And soon Ramsey is offered a terrible deal, one that could save or destroy the entire town, and maybe even the world.

Also by Amy Cross

Asylum
(The Asylum Trilogy book 1)

"No-one ever leaves Lakehurst. The staff, the patients, the ghosts... Once you're here, you're stuck forever."

After shooting her little brother dead, Annie Radford is sent to Lakehurst psychiatric hospital for assessment. Hearing voices in her head, Annie is forced to undergo experimental new treatments devised by a mysterious old man who lives in the hospital's attic. It soon becomes clear that the hospital's staff, led by the vicious Nurse Winter, are hiding something horrific at Lakehurst.

As Annie struggles to survive the hospital, she learns more about Nurse Winter's own story. Once a promising young medical student, Kirsten Winter also heard voices in her head. Voices that traveled a long way to reach her. Voices that have a plan of their own. Voices that will stop at nothing to get what they want.

What kind of signals are being transmitted from the basement of the hospital? Who is the old man in the attic? Why are living human brains kept in jars? And what is the dark secret that lurks at the heart of the hospital?

Also by Amy Cross

The Ghost of Molly Holt

"Molly Holt is dead. There's nothing to fear in this house."

When three teenagers set out to explore an abandoned house in the middle of a forest, they think they've found the location where the infamous Molly Holt video was filmed.

They've found much more than that...

Tim doesn't believe in ghosts, but he has a crush on a girl who does. That's why he ends up taking her out to the house, and it's also why he lets her take his only flashlight. But as they explore the house together, Tim and Becky start to realize that something else might be lurking in the shadows.

Something that, ten years ago, suffered unimaginable pain.

Something that won't rest until a terrible wrong has been put right.

For more information, visit:

www. amycross.com

34120380R00118

Printed in Great Britain
by Amazon